A Ratchet City Celebration

A Ratchet City Goon's Thanksgiving Celebration
By
Renessa Jackson

Table of Contents

CHAPTER ONE THE BREAKING POINT 1
CHAPTER TWO A FRESH ENCOUNTER 18
CHAPTER THREE UNWANTED DRAMA 31
CHAPTER FOUR LEGEND'S FALL 42
CHAPTER FIVE NEW ALLIANCES 51
CHAPTER SIX FINDING HERSELF AGAIN 60
CHAPTER SEVEN OPENING UP 70
CHAPTER EIGHT THE COLLEGE DREAM 75
CHAPTER NINE COREY'S REALITY CHECK 81
CHAPTER TEN COREY'S FINAL STUNT 87
CHAPTER ELEVEN THANKSGIVING CELEBRATION WITH FRIENDS 91
NOTE TO READER 96
WHAT'S NEXT ON YOUR READING LIST? 97
STAY CONNECTED 111
CONNECT ON SOCIAL 112
ABOUT THE AUTHOR 113
ABOUT THE PUBLISHER 114
ACKNOWLEDGEMENT 115

OTHER TITLES BY AUTHOR

Luvin a Young Ratchet City Boss

Luvin a Young Ratchet City Boss 3rd EDITION

A Ratchet City Hustler's Unexpected Halloween Surprise

COPYRIGHT

COPYRIGHT© 2024 A Ratchet City Goon's Thanksgiving Celebration by Renessa D. Jackson. Unless otherwise indicated, all materials on these pages are copyrighted by Allure Productions LLC. All rights reserved. No part of these pages, either text or image may be used for any purpose other than personal use. Therefore, reproduction, modification, in any form or by any means, electronic, mechanical or otherwise, for reasons other than personal use, is strictly prohibited without prior written permission from the publisher and writer, except brief quotes used in reviews. This is a work of fiction. Any references or similarities to actual events, real people, living or dead, or to the real locals intend to give the novel a sense of reality. Any similarity in other names, characters, places, and incidents are entirely coincidental.

TABLE OF CONTENTS

OTHER TITLES BY AUTHOR

COPYRIGHT

CHAPTER ONE THE BREAKING POINT

REFLECTIONS OF WASTED LOVE

CHAPTER TWO A FRESH ENCOUNTER

CHAPTER THREE UNWANTED DRAMA

CHAPTER FOUR LEGEND'S FALL

CHAPTER FIVE NEW ALLIANCES

CHAPTER SIX FINDING HERSELF AGAIN

CHAPTER SEVEN OPENING UP

CHAPTER EIGHT THE COLLEGE DREAM

CHAPTER NINE COREY'S FINAL STUNT

CHAPTER TEN THANKSGIVING CELEBRATION WITH FRIENDS

NOTE TO READER

WHAT'S NEXT ON YOUR READING LIST?

STAY CONNECTED

CONNECT ON SOCIAL

ABOUT THE AUTHOR

ABOUT THE PUBLISHER

ACKNOWLEDGEMENT

CHAPTER ONE THE BREAKING POINT

I stomped down the cracked sidewalk of Milam Street, frustrated beyond belief. My heart was pounding so fast in my chest, causing me to move with a sense of urgency. My hourglass figure and tiny waist curved out to thick thighs and a round behind, and it was catching attention even in my anger. My long curly hair bounced past my shoulders and my baby face, big doe eyes and full lips stayed pretty even twisted up in fury.

The sun was blazing high over Ratchet City, despite it being late October. It was beating down hard on everything, this bipolar weather making me wonder why I even bothered to wear a jacket. The way it's hitting I have sweat beaded across my forehead, but the heat I feel most predominately is coming from the fury I have boiling inside me. Fury at myself mostly because I felt pathetic for dealing with Corey's bullshit.

But this was just another typical day for me since I've been fucking around with Corey. It wasn't just the suffocating humidity of the Louisiana afternoon. It was the rage, the uncontainable anger, the feeling of betrayal that has me seething. It was my conscience beating me up for being so stupid. Here it is yet another occasion that people are blowing up my phone telling me that Corey was up at the barbershop with Teresa. The same Teresa that I have caught him foolin' around with on three other occasions.

I rounded the corner of Pierre Avenue at 'Foot's Automotive & Car Detail Shop' and stopped dead in my tracks at the sight of them posted up in the back corner of the 'Fresh2Def87 Barber & Beauty Shop'. I could clearly make them out kissing for everyone to see through the wide front window.

Pokey, that's what everybody called Byron Allen, had his shop decked out with vibrant red-and-black on the walls where the barber's and stylist's chairs were covered in matching tones. At 5'9" and built like a linebacker, Pokey's broad shoulders filled out his fitted Polo button-up nice and his thick tatted arms led down to large hands that handled his clippers with precision. He stayed fresh to death now wearing the new Jordan 4s coupled with designer jeans with the perfect crease. And his platinum watch, rings, and chains was catching light with his every move. So, the colors inside the shop gave it a fresh look that compliments its owner's style.

I walked in and the air inside smelled of hair products, spicy cologne, and the ever-present aroma of hot hair tools. Barbers and stylists worked at their chairs on clients, each station cluttered with clippers, combs, and sprays, while there was music blasting from the speakers mounted in every corner of the shop. The bass thumped through the space, blending with the buzzing of clippers and the rhythmic chatter coming from the other clients and two local hood celebrity's named Rondicious "RonB" Davis and Glen "PNUT" Bryant. They were busy shooting dice over in the corner of the shop not paying me any mind.

I just stood there shaking my head and watching the two of them standing at the far end of the shop. Fucking Corey Anderson. My Corey, supposably. All 5'7" of him with his plain features that wasn't ugly but wasn't nothing special either, slim built with no muscle tone despite all the hours he claimed to spend at the gym. And his ass stayed dripping in jewelry. Right now, he's wearing a Cuban link chain with two diamond tennis chains layered underneath. Both of his wrists were shining with two Cartier bracelets I helped him get, and every finger weighed down with gold rings. The nigga who had promised me the world, who had whispered dreams of forever to me was standing there with his hands wrapped around Teresa Wilkins's waist. His lips was pressed against hers in a kiss so deep and shameless that it sent a wave of nausea crashing over me just looking at the two of them.

Teresa was posted up against Corey looking like she just walked out of Dillard's, with her slim-thick frame poured into her tight Fendi leggings and the matching top. She kept bouncing her leg making her Red bottoms click against the floor and that red Birkin bag she's always bragging about was sitting on the counter (probably fake like everything else about her), with a fresh silk press laying perfect, and her ever present long designer nails wrapped around My man's neck.

A RATCHET CITY GOON'S THANKSGIVING CELEBRATION

Then there was the laughter and whispers rippling through the shop from the other clients looking at me mockingly. Their conversations instantly dropped to hushed tones. Their eyes darting back and forth between Corey and I. It was all a hot ass mess. A spectacle. The kind that I seem to always be the fool at the center of and I was fed the fuck up.

"*Wow.*" I whispered.

"*Dee, what you doing here?*" Pokey called out from behind his chair, setting down his clippers, he walked towards me. Over the years owning this shop he's seen all kinds of drama go down.

I was so preoccupied I ain't even answer him. My eyes locked on Corey and Teresa as a murderous rage overtook my vision.

"*Girl, you might wanna handle this outside,*" Teresa's friend Anna whispered, trying to pull me back. "*This ain't the place.*"

"*Nah,*" I said, shrugging her off. "*Let everybody see. I'm tired of him and his bullshit. We may as well go out with a bang, don't you think?*"

The shop got quiet real quick, except for RonB, PNUT, and the others shouting out sporadically and the R&B playing overhead. That's when Corey finally noticed me standing there, his eyes going wide as he tried to push Teresa aside.

His mouth opening to form words, but what the fuck was he supposed to say. I caught his ass with his tongue down this hoe's throat. This ain't no "*mistake,*" no "*misunderstanding,*" and his bitch ass ain't "*confused.*" If he can't tell me and this hoe apart he needs to get glasses or an eye transplant. Besides I ain't interested in hearing any more of his lies.

"*Really Nigga,*" I said, my voice carrying across the shop. "*You just can't help yourself, can you? You couldn't even pretend to have the slightest bit of respect for me, could you? But you know what? The fourth time's the charm, Corey. We're done.*"

Teresa smirked, leaning against Corey as if she belonged there. And maybe she did. I seem to be the one out of place here, and for the first time in five years, I'm good with that. These hoe's can have this nigga. I'm done.

"*Oh, look, it's Little Miss Doormat. Ain't you tired of running up behind Corey? Damn, you ain't his mama.*" She mocked smirking, voice dripping with contempt, as she struggled trying to press herself closer to Corey. Her eyes lit with a challenge I was more than ready to accept. Today this bitch got the right one.

My hands balled into fists at my sides as I took a breath trying to get a hold on my anger. The last thing I needed was to be out here fighting over this lame ass nigga. It took me five years. Five years of listening to his lies, of feeling small and stupid every time I forgave him. Five years of losing myself, of distancing myself from my friends and pretending things would get better.

My anger twisted into a physical ache, and I wanted to scream at and slap the shit out of my 12 year old self for letting me waste so much of my time on this nothing ass nigga. Corey in no way deserved me. Nigga got me feeling like Keyshia Cole, thinking *"I shoulda cheated."*

"Dee, come on now. You know it's not what it looks like..." Corey stepped forward, his voice coming out soft in a clumsy attempt at damage control.

"Nigga, not what it looks like? I just saw you wit' yo' tongue down this hoe's throat." I spat, my voice cracking with hurt and fury. *"You say the same bullshit every time I catch you cheating, Corey. Every. Single. Time. I'm done with your lies. I'm done with your cheating. But most important, I'm done with you."*

"Girl, please. If you were really done, you wouldn't keep coming back. We all know you can't leave Corey alone." Teresa laughed at me, a high, disdainful sound that grated on my last nerve.

Then the laughter of the shop's other patrons cut into my skin like shards of glass, each snicker amplifying my already unsurmountable humiliation. I turned to face Teresa, my vision blurring with rage.

"First off, bitch," I stepped forward, *"I ain't talkin' to yo' hoe ass and don't speak to me unless you're spoken to. I'm trying to spare you because you don't ole me nothing. Corey cheated so my beef is with him, but if you keep testing me like it's a game. Umma show you something funny."*

"Dee, baby, listen..." Corey tried to step between us, his chains jingling with every move.

"Nah, you listen," I cut him off. *"Five years I gave you. Five years of second chances, of believing your lies, of looking stupid in front of everybody. And I'm done. D-O-N-E, done."*

"Please," Teresa rolled her eyes, her fake lashes fluttering. *"You'll be back next week like always."*

A RATCHET CITY GOON'S THANKSGIVING CELEBRATION

"*That's where you're wrong,*" I laughed, but there wasn't no humor in it. "*See, I finally figured something out, you and this nigga are perfect for each other. Two, two-timing, lying, ain't got no respect having individuals. A match made in heaven. So, you can have this nigga. Enjoy!*"

"*You don't mean that,*" Corey reached for my hand but I snatched it back, the gold rings on his hands flashing in the light.

"*Don't I? When's the last time you was honest with me, Corey? When's the last time you showed me any real respect?*" I could feel tears trying to come but I pushed them back. "*I'm better than this and I deserve better than this bullshit. I deserve better than you. I shoulda left your ass a long time ago.*"

"*Girl, if you was better, he wouldn't keep coming to me,*" Teresa started, adjusting the designer purse on her shoulder, but Pokey cut her off.

"*Teresa, you might wanna sit down somewhere,*" he warned, stepping out from behind his chair, the mats squeaking against the clean floor under his weight. "*This ain't that kind of shop, and you ain't helping nothing.*"

"*Wait Pokey,*" I stopped him and turned to address her. "*Teresa what's your deal? 'Cause I find it crazy that you keep coming for me. Do you talk just to hear yourself talk? The shit you're sayin' is not makin' any sense. I'm not holdin' Corey hostage. Believe me when I say he can go be with whomever he wants. He's free. In fact, I just set him free in front of you. Why are you on me like you're gay?*" I asked, perplexed. "*Cause if you are, I'm sorry honey. I'm strictly dickly.*"

"*The fuck you tryin' to say?*" Corey snapped acting offended. "*You going too far Dee.*"

Teresa stepped forward, her eyes narrowing to slits.

"*Bitch, I ain't gay. You're just trying to deflect. What I think is, you should learn to handle your man, or someone else will,*" she scoffed, lifting her hand to spread out in front of my face.

That was it for me. The last thread of my restraint snapped. My thick thighs powered me forward as I lunged at Teresa, my fist connecting with the side of her jaw. The fake lashes on her eyes went flying as my knuckles hit her jaw under her eye. The shop erupted into chaos, chairs scraping against the floor as people scrambled to get out of the way.

"*Stop Dee! What are you doing?*" Corey had the nerve to shout at me, his gold chains swinging as he tried to grab my arm, but I wasn't having it. I'm tired of this hoe picking with me.

"*The fuck y'all got going on over there?*" RonB shouted.

"*Pokey the fuck kinda shit you allowing 'round here? You tryna have the pigs run up in this bitch or what?*" PNUT fired off.

I ain't pay none of what was going on around me no mind. I was determined to make this hoe feel me, "*Bitch, this ass whippin' ain't about Corey's hoe ass. It's about the disrespect you continue to show towards me. If you want this nigga, go get him, but like I said, keep my name out your mouth.*" I punctuated each word by punching her in the face, watching her designer outfit get ruined with blood stains as she stumbled back into Pokey's station.

"*Not in my shop!*" Pokey's deep voice boomed across the space, his stocky frame trying to move through the crowd to get to us. Most of the clients took out their phones videoing the fight. "*Y'all need to take this shit outside!*"

I ignored Pokey, concentrating on rearranging her face. Teresa tried to block access to her face by curling up in a ball, but I was relentless, punching every piece of skin I had access to.

"*When you see me hoe, go the other way, 'cause every time I see you from now on, it's on sight. Umma give you the ass whippins' yo' mammy should have given you. Keep playin' wit' me.*"

All the pain, the humiliation, the guilt, the bitterness... it all came pouring out in a flurry of punches and kicks. My long curls whipping around as I smashed that hoe's face in. She was bleeding from her nose, lips, and had a swollen eye. The red bottoms on her feet ain't help her none, she couldn't fight back, couldn't land not one punch. I had 5 years of pinned up anger and I let her have it all.

"*Get off me! Somebody get her off of me,*" Teresa begged, her slim-thick frame crumpling under my assault. "*Get this crazy bitch off of me!*"

"*Nah, I ain't crazy,*" I growled, "*Just done with the bullshit!*"

"*Nawl! Say it ain't so? I know bad ass Teresa Wilkins ain't begging after all the shit you just talked.*" PNUT taunted.

"*Yeah, after all that big talk you had just a minute ago, I know your bad ass ain't in here beggin' for help.*" RonB mocked, and the shop erupted into laughter.

The fight got messy. I gave her dozens of fists and knees to her body, and Teresa's screams echoed through the shop. I didn't care that she was bloody or that my baby face was twisted with rage while the fresh press on my hair was getting sweated out. I didn't care whether she was in tears or that snot was

A RATCHET CITY GOON'S THANKSGIVING CELEBRATION

streaming down her face. All I could feel was the raw, unfiltered rage that had built up over five years due to Corey's betrayal. And I wanted my licks back.

"*Deandra, that's enough!*" Pokey's voice cut through again, but I wasn't finished.

"*Shit, let her finish. This hoe need this ass whipping. It'll teach her to keep her legs and mouth closed.*" RonB jabbed.

"*Yeah, Pokey. Let Dee handle her business. This hoe been pickin' a while. I guess Dee finally got tired.*" PNUT endorsed.

"*How could I have been so stupid?*" I ranted to myself, even as my fist kept swinging forward. "*Five years. Five fuckin' years of believing in him, of forgiving him, of thinking he'd change. I gave up my friends, my peace, my happiness, and for what? It couldn't be for this. I refuse to accept that.*" I vented as I continued to punch her in the face.

Once I eased up, Teresa tried to use her long designer nails to claw at my face, but I shoved her back. "*Bitch move,*" I spat, slappin' her across the face. The Birkin bag she'd just retrieved from the counter went flying, contents spilling everywhere.

"*Look what the fuck y'all did to my shop!*" Pokey roared. "*Y'all done destroyed my shit! Somebody better be ready to pay for all this!*"

"*Send the bill to Corey,*" I snapped back. "*Since he wanna be playin' both sides!*"

"*Hell nah,*" Corey protested, adjusting his chains. "*I ain't paying for shit! This between y'all!*"

"*Nigga, if you don't pay to fix my shit,*" Pokey stepped to him, using every inch of his 5'9" frame to tower over Corey's 5'7", "*you and your little jewelry collection I been letting you sale out of here ain't welcome back. Period.*"

"*Yeah, Nigga. You the reason Dee up here in this predicament anyway. All you got to do is sell a couple chains to cover the cost.*" PNUT reasoned.

"*If not, you can get the money how you live, but Dee ain't payin' for shit. This yo' fuck up.*" RonB affirmed.

I was breathing hard. I hate that I let Corey and this bitch get me out of character. I let him make me feel like I wasn't good enough. Like I had to keep proving myself to his punk ass, keep forgiving him, just to be proved wrong over and over again.

"Look at my shop," Pokey surveyed the damage. "Two chairs broke, mirror cracked, products everywhere. Corey you need to be cutting a check today."

"I got you," Teresa wiped blood from her face, pulling out her phone. "But she attacked me. I'm pressing charges!"

"Press whatever you want," I squared up again. "I'll catch another charge."

"Ain't nobody pressing nothing," Pokey declared. "Teresa you wrote a check your ass couldn't cash and got handled. How you gone be cheating wit' this nigga and talkin' shit to his lady when y'all get caught. Take that ass whippin' and keep it movin'. We don't play them pig games 'round here. But that aside. I need the money for my shop, now."

"Sure, the fuck ain't. The fuck you calling the cops for when you begged for that ass whipping?" PNUT spazzed.

"Dee ain't say shit to you. She stepped to her man. You the one who inserted yourself into their business with all that extra shit you had to say. Dee was within her rights to tag your ass. You ain't bringing no cops 'round here making our spot hot. Get the fuck outta here wit' that bullshit." RonB spat.

I was grateful for their support, but I was done with it all. I turned back to Corey one last time.

"I hope she was worth it. I hope she was worth you losing the only person who really gave a damn about your hoe ass. Cause I'm out. For good this time. Delete my number, lose my address, forget my name. We're done."

I walked out that shop with my head held high, ignoring the whispers and stares. Five years of drama ending right there in Fresh2Def87. But for the first time in forever, I felt light. Free. Ready to love myself, show respect in myself, and improve myself.

Behind me, I could hear Teresa's heels clicking as she started yappin' again, but this time her ire was aimed at Corey, asking him why he didn't help her. Both PNUT and RonB told her he didn't help because he knew they'd break his fuckin' neck. Their voices grew faint with every step I took. I let her have Corey. Some nigga's ain't worth fighting over, and Corey Anderson definitely ain't no prize to be out here breaking my nails over, no matter how much jewelry he was wearing. He ain't worth shit. Too bad it took my stupid ass five long years to figure that out.

A RATCHET CITY GOON'S THANKSGIVING CELEBRATION

REFLECTIONS OF WASTED LOVE

AFTER THAT FIGHT WITH Teresa, my body was still shaking with adrenaline and my thick thighs were trembling since I walked until I found myself at Lakeside Park. I ended up sitting on the small bench where me and Corey's lying ass made so many memories over the years. The bright autumn leaves fell softly around me, dancing in the breeze catching my attention despite my whole world crumbling. The park was quiet except for the distant sound of the guys playing basketball, their chains and jewelry jingling with every shot.

"*Five fucking years,*" I gritted bitterly, my baby face twisted in pain spreading across my cute features.

I was staring out over the vacant baseball field, my long curly hair whipping in the wind. I was trying my best to hold it together, but damn. I spent five years giving everything I had to a nothing ass nigga who gave me nothing but heartbreak in return. The weight of my past choices felt so suffocating, like somebody was sitting on my chest. Every breath I took came in slow, sharp pants like I swallowed broken glass. It was a struggle to take a deep breath 'cause the air kept biting into my lungs. But nothing could overshadow the regret and self-crimination that raged inside my soul.

"*I was a complete fool for Corey,*" I screamed into the empty park, hoping the release would relieve some of my misery. My hourglass figure shook with each sob I tried to hold back.

My memories pulled me back, replaying the endless parade of betrayals like a horror flick I couldn't turn off. My jaw tightened remembering how young and naïve I'd been the first time I caught Corey cheating with Betty Smith behind the bleachers at J.S. Clark Middle School. Betty with her light skin and box braids, always wearing Baby Phat jeans and thinking she was all that.

I had been on my way to deliver Corey a surprise lunch during recess. I used my allowance to get his favorite burger from the food truck near school. So, I had come looking for him with a hopeful smile, only to find him wrapped around Betty, laughing like his plain-faced ass didn't have a girlfriend.

Betty's small hands were clutching his hoodie as they laughed between their secret kisses. I stood there frozen, my heart splintering, but Corey's apology...

"*His tearful, puppy-dog-eyed promise that he'd made a 'mistake' had wormed its way into my heart and I forgave him.*" I grunted, my lips curling in disgust.

"Shoulda known then that his puppy-dog eyes was just as fake as the jewelry he be wearing now."

I was only twelve, and I thought it was just a childish mistake.

"Twelve years old and already learning how to accept less than I deserve," I muttered, kicking at the fallen leaves.

"I should have known better, even then. I should have walked away," I scolded myself. *"But nah, my dumb ass stayed. Thinking I could fix a broke nigga who ain't want fixing."*

But I didn't leave. I had clung to the hope that he could change, that my love would be enough to fix him.

"That was so very naïve of me, because guess what? The cycle of cheating, lies, and betrayal had only gotten worse." I vented to myself as more memories hit.

"Then there was Cynthia Allen," I hissed, clutching my fists until my nails bit into my palms. *"Miss Track Star with her long legs and attitude bigger than her talent."*

Cynthia had brazenly flaunted Corey in front of the whole school. Posted him up on her social media with the caption *'My man crush every day.'* Looking like a whole clown in the matching outfits she made them wear in the photo.

"And don't get me started on Sheila Fletcher," I growled. *"Always showing up to school in the designer fits her mama bought her, acting bougie despite living in the same projects as the rest of us."*

I caught him with Sheila in the back of his cousin's beat-up car during a house party. That scene still haunted me, the music blaring, and laughter spilling out from the house. I spotted them wrapped up together, and for a moment, I couldn't breathe. My girls, Raylexia and Johnya, found me sobbing on the curb.

Raylexia, with her striking silver hair and her rare violet eyes, had grabbed my shoulders. Her voice echoed in my mind.

"Dee, please, leave that boy alone. He's poison and if you don't get away from him, you're gonna end up infected with something you can't get rid of. We're here for you. We've got your back, just let him go. There are better guys out there that will treat you right," she'd begged.

Bitterness coiled in my gut, making me realize just how hardheaded I'd been in regard to Corey's cheating. I was obstinate and wouldn't listen to

A RATCHET CITY GOON'S THANKSGIVING CELEBRATION

reason. The autumn wind whipped around me, my body shivering on that cold park bench where I used to think life was perfect.

"I hate him for wasting my time," I rasped, my voice rough from crying. "For making me believe I wasn't good enough with all this," I gestured at my thick thighs, tiny waist, and curves that other girls wish they had, "and that I had to earn his loyalty. But I hate myself more. I hate that I let him get close enough to do it."

The basketball court behind me echoed with shouts and laughter, reminding me of all the games I missed watching my girls play just to sit around waiting on Corey's lying ass.

"I wanted to believe him more than I wanted to face the truth." I wheezed out a shaky breath, my voice barely above a whisper. A lump formed in my throat, and no matter how hard I tried to push it down, it stayed stuck, stubborn like my damn pride.

The memories were relentless, each one cutting deeper than the last. I gripped the edge of the park bench, my knuckles turning white as I fought to keep myself from drowning in the flood of painful flashbacks.

"Daisy McNeil," I muttered, squeezing my eyes shut, trying to block out the humiliation that still burned hot. The name alone was enough to make my skin crawl. "Daisy had been bold with it, too. I'd walked into the basketball game, grinning and waving at folks like I was untouchable, only to catch Corey locking lips with her right there in front of everyone. The whispers had hit me first, low and sharp, and then the laughter cut through me like a blade. I couldn't escape the smirks, the side-eyes, the pity. That moment wasn't just about Corey and Daisy; it felt like the whole crowd had been in on the joke. My heartbreak had become entertainment."

"Corey swore up and down he was "confused," said he didn't know what he wanted. Promised me he'd make it right."

"Confused?" I sneered, the word tasting bitter as it left my mouth. "It was nothin' but more lies. All lies, but my stupid ass just kept on believing them." My voice cracked, and I felt the heat rising in my chest.

"Then came Alanna," I spat. Damn, Alanna Williamson, with her long nails clicking against her phone and her lip gloss always poppin'. "I'd walked into the arcade with my girls, laughing about some nonsense, feeling good for the first time in a minute. Then the mood shifted. Their smiles faded, replaced by those "I'm sorry, girl" expressions that made my stomach drop. I turned, following their eyes, and there she was, bold as hell, sitting in Corey's lap like she belonged there. She had the nerve to smirk at me, her manicured finger tracing circles on his chest like she was marking her territory. Rage took over, and before I knew it, my hand connected with Corey's face, the slap echoing loud enough to make everyone stop and stare."

Even then, I stayed. I stayed and turned my anger on Corey, not because I believed his excuses, but because I couldn't face the truth. The real fight wasn't with him or Alanna or any of the other girls; it was with myself. My constant forgiveness, my constant denial, my constant inability to just let him go.

"The roster of girls seemed endless," I sighed. "Each name hit like a slap I never saw coming. Pamela Reed, with her loud laugh and curves that could make traffic stop; Felicia Mitchell, always "innocent" until you caught her in the act; Helen Wright, who bragged about her "little secret" to anyone who would listen; and Sonja Hawkins, who wore heartbreak like a badge of honor but still thought she could play me."

"And those were just the ones I caught," I grunted, miserable. "There were others, the whispers, the rumors. The girl from the mall who wore Corey's hoodie like a trophy. The one from the block party who swayed a little too close to him during the 'Cupid Shuffle.' The cashier at the corner store who always added extra items to his bag with a wink."

With every new name, every new betrayal, a piece of me broke off. It wasn't just the cheating; it was the disrespect, the way he could look me in the eyes and lie without blinking. By the time I caught him with Sonja, I was numb. My girls had stopped repeating themselves, tired of reminding me of what I already knew but couldn't accept.

My thoughts drifted to the sorrow I carried over missed opportunities. There had been boys who had tried to get my attention. Like quiet, sweet Darien Williams, with his clean fade and entrepreneur mind, already running his own car detailing business at seventeen, who had slipped me a love note in eighth grade. And kind-hearted Gearld Taylor, tall, dark, and fine with his dimples that made all the teachers smile, who had wanted to take me to homecoming. I had stupidly turned them all down, convinced that Corey's basic looking self was the only one for me.

A RATCHET CITY GOON'S THANKSGIVING CELEBRATION

"*What if I missed out on real love?*" I mocked myself, my face twisted in disgust. "*What if someone could have treated me like the queen I am while I was hanging on to that bottom-shelf nigga?*"

But the worry that cut me deepest was about my friends. My day ones. My real ones. I had pushed them away to be with Corey, and I feared that bridge was burned beyond repair.

"*Melissa Johnson,*" I spat the name like poison, remembering another one of Corey's conquests. "*That light-skinned, red-bone thinking she all that 'cause her daddy owned the corner store. Always showing up to school with fresh Nike's and attitude.*"

I thought back to that day in the hallway at Booker T. Washington High. Johnya had confronted me, her golden honey skin glowing with anger, her voice tinged with frustration.

"*Dee, I saw him with Melissa. They was all over each other at the library. That nigga's not worth your tears,*" Johnya had snapped.

"*You're wrong, Johnya. You don't know him like I do. He promised me.*" I had shaken my head, eyes glistening like a straight fool.

"*Nah, you don't know him,*" Raylexia had cut in, her silver hair catching light like diamonds, her violet eyes blazing with fury. "*Are you stuck on stupid or what? Dee, you better open your fuckin' eyes. That nigga's playing you, and we're tired of watching you get hurt.*"

"*My girls,*" I whispered now, my hair falling forward to hide my tears. "*My real ones who been there since elementary, who braided my hair for free when I ain't have money for the salon, who snuck me food when mama was working late shifts.*"

"*I threw away sisterhood for a fuck boy,*" I choked out, the shame burning hotter than any Louisiana summer. "*Left my girls hanging dry while I was chasing behind a nigga who wouldn't even claim me in public unless his other girls wasn't around.*"

The memory of Raylexia and the girl's birthday hit different now.

"*My best friends since fifth grade,*" I whispered, guilt crushing my chest. "*I missed their fourteenth birthday celebration 'cause Corey said he had something special planned. I ended up sitting in my room alone while he was probably out with another female.*"

"Ain't that some shit?" I laughed bitterly. "Every time the girls had something planned, Winkie's side jobs doing home decorations, Johnya's baby shower for Tylan, and Shamena's jobs doing hair for events in groups. It never missed that Corey would come through with his lies. And stupid me, thinking I was chosen, would ditch my real ones for his fake ass."

"I done messed up bad," I whispered into the wind, watching leaves scatter across the baseball field. "Five years of choosing an ain't shit nigga over my real friends. The same girls who had my back since we was sharing our lunch in elementary."

My mind drifted to Shamena, with her deep ebony skin that looked like pure silk in the sun, always rocking her hair in natural twists and speaking life into everybody she met.

"Remember when Shamena got her cosmetology license the first year of high school?" I asked myself, guilt eating at my soul. "The first one of us to establish a legitimate way to generate income honestly. She caused the rest of the girls to get their license in the various types of body enhancement fields. Johnya does massage and facials, Winkie does wax, Deana does nails, and Raylexia does brows and management. And they had a whole celebration dinner planned..."

My chest got tight remembering how I'd texted last minute to cancel. "Sorry girl, Corey surprised me with tickets to the concert..." I could still see her response: "It's cool, Dee. We'll celebrate with you another time." But we never did.

Then there was Winkie/Shayla but nobody called her that since middle school. She has a 5'7" tall frame that's slim and curvy with the perfect eyebrows over beautiful gray eyes. My girl has been doing design since she got old enough to match colors.

"Winkie did her first home design project for King Michael a major dealer in the area, and she requested we all help," I croaked, tears falling. "I was all set to go, leaving out the door with Raylexia...Corey called to say he wanted to take me to the movie and was on his way to pick me up."

I turned to Raylexia to explain, but she cut me off before I could speak... "I already know. I'll explain it to Winkie." I rushed back inside to quickly change, only to end up sitting around looking stupid 'cause Corey never showed up.

"They had their first performance at the Belvins' Brother's Spar Basketball Tournament," I sobbed, a fresh batch of tears falling. "They gave me front row seats saved for their friends and family... and my chair sat empty 'cause Corey said

A RATCHET CITY GOON'S THANKSGIVING CELEBRATION

he needed me that night. Turned out he was at the movies with Keisha Williams, some chick with a fake everything and slept around with all the guys."

"Damn," I cursed, my hands shaking as I wiped my face. *"Every time I chose him, I lost a piece of myself. Lost the Deandra who used to be a shoulder for my friends to cry on. The friend who'd fight somebody for looking at her girls wrong."*

"Girl, we don't even know who you are anymore. Used to be you'd run through the school hallways ready to throw hands if somebody tried your friends. Now you sitting quiet while Corey and his little hoes laugh in your face." Johnya's words from freshmen year cut me deep.

"My girl Deana just like Shamena got her cosmetology license for nails right after Shamena," I remembered, *"The celebration with everybody coming. The whole family cooking and celebrating... and I missed it 'cause Corey said he wanted to 'take me out to dinner.'"* I scoffed. *"Dinner my ass. He was probably somewhere laid up with Jessica Thomas, that wannabe model who stayed scamming dudes for a few rags."* That was the memory of Deana's graduation party and it made my gut twist.

"And Raylexia..." My voice cracked on her name. My best friend since we was learning our first math equations. Her with that rare silver hair that everybody thought was fake and her violet eyes that had people asking if she was wearing contacts. *"She tried the hardest to save me from myself."*

The park around me was getting darker, street lights flickering on one by one. A couple walked past holding hands, reminding me of all the real love I'd pushed away for fake promises.

"Remember when Ray's grandma's death anniversary came?" I asked the empty air. *"She called crying, needing her best friends... and what did I do? Let Corey convince me he was sick and needed me to nurse him. Meanwhile Ray was at the grave site with Rod, Deana, Johnya, Shamena, and Winkie, thinking I had abandoned her."*

"Fuck!" I slammed my fist against the bench. *"How many times did I leave my girls hanging? How many moments can I never get back?"*

I jumped up and paced the space in front of the bench, my sneakers scuffing against the grass. The area around me felt like it was closing in on me, trapping me with my thoughts. The park had gone quiet, too still, but inside me. It was chaos. A storm of anger, sadness, and shame that I couldn't quiet no matter how hard I tried.

"*Why?*" I asked the empty park, my voice trembling. "*Why did I keep takin' him back? Was it love? Was it fear? Or was it just that I didn't know how to be without him?*"

I sat back down on the bench, burying my face in my hands. The truth was, Corey wasn't just a person. He was a habit, a toxic cycle I didn't know how to break. Loving him had become second nature, even when it hurt.

My friends tried to help me break the cycle, "*Raylexia with her no-nonsense advice, Deana with her quiet support, Shamena with her sharp tongue, Winkie with her voice of reason, and Johnya with her planned sneak attacks, all of them ready to throw hands if it came to that.*" I mused, thinking about all the times and ways they tried to pull me out of it. "*They'd warned me, begged me to see the truth, but I'd been too blind, too stubborn.*"

The group chat notification still blinked on my phone. More than a year of ignored messages, missed birthdays, forgotten celebrations. My fingers trembled as I scrolled through old texts.

"*We miss you Dee,*" Johnya had written sixteen months ago.

"*Still got your hair gel whenever you ready,*" from Shamena.

"*Saw your mama at the store. She said you're doing good. Wish you'd tell us yourself,*" Deana wrote.

"*Remember when we used to have breakfast before school at Raylexia's place? Rod, Reign, and Tonya still ask about you,*" from Winkie.

"*Your spot in the sister circle still open whenever you're ready to come home,*" Ray's last message read.

"*Home,*" I repeated, my heart aching. "*There with them was my real home. My safe space. My backbone. And I traded all that love for a nigga who couldn't even be faithful while I was helping him pay his phone bill.*"

Looking up at the darkening sky, city lights twinkling overhead, I made a promise to myself. "*If they give me another chance,*" I whispered fiercely, "*I'm gonna spend the rest of my life making up for lost time. Gonna be the friend they deserve. The sister they need. The Deandra I used to be before I let a fuck boy dim my light.*"

"*Not gonna happen no more,*" I whispered to myself, the words like a vow. "*I ain't lettin' him drag me back in no more.*"

The air felt heavy, like the calm before a storm. But this time, I wasn't waiting for Corey to bring the thunder. I was gonna find my own strength, my

A RATCHET CITY GOON'S THANKSGIVING CELEBRATION

own peace. And if he thought he could waltz back into my life with another apology and a promise he couldn't keep, he had another thing comin'.

My hands still shaking, I opened the group chat again. After five years of choosing to do the wrong thing. Of missing moments with my friends. Of breaking life long bonds. But maybe, just maybe, it wasn't too late for me to come back home. Back to the people who really cared about me and my wellbeing.

"*Girls...*" I typed, then deleted. My heart was pounding so hard my chest hurt. *"I know I don't deserve it... but I miss my sisters..."*

For the first time in what felt like forever, I let the tears fall. Not for Corey, not for the girls, but for me, for the pieces of myself I'd lost along the way. And as the tears dried, something inside me shifted. I wasn't broken. I was just starting to rebuild.

CHAPTER TWO A FRESH ENCOUNTER

The late afternoon sun dipped low in the sky, casting a golden glow over the red-brick buildings of the Jackson Heights projects. The black iron fences shimmered like they'd been polished, standing guard around the complex alive with energy. Music thumped from somebody's speakers, bass rattling through the walls, while the mingling smells of fried fish, seasoned chicken, and various other foods somebody's cooking floated out through open windows. The freshly cut grass added a sharp greenness to the air, and my stomach twisted at the mix of smells, though I hadn't been eating much lately.

Not since my fallout with Corey. I've been too busy tryna figure out my next moves to reclaim my life. So much of what I did from day to day was decided by Corey. The thought of him alone made my jaw tighten. For five years, my life had revolved around his lies, his schemes, his controlling ways. Now, with him out of the picture, I was finally free, but freedom was heavier than I expected. I didn't even know how to start putting the pieces of me back together. I kept telling myself to focus on getting a better job, saving up some money, and enrolling at the University of Shreveport for the next semester. But for now, I was stuck making minimum wage at McDonald's, barely helping my mom keep the bills paid. It in no way provides me with what I need to be able to be truly independent.

Shaking off that train of thought I walked over to collect our mail. The hollow clang of the communal mailboxes echoed as I leaned against the side of the laundry building. My thick hips rested against the concrete wall, my fingers fumbling with the small silver key as I tried to distract myself from my fucked up disposition. It's been so long since I was free to do whatever without Corey's

A RATCHET CITY GOON'S THANKSGIVING CELEBRATION

lying ass watching my every move, that I chose to stay alone in our apartment, just trying to get my head right.

The sound of kids playing in *"The Field"* filled the air, shrieks of laughter, the rhythmic scrape of sneakers on concrete, and the occasional *"Aye, pass it here!"* Their joy felt so foreign to me, almost like I didn't deserve to feel it myself. Years of Corey's bullshit had turned my days gray, and now that I had my freedom, I didn't even know what happiness felt like.

Just as I wrestled the stubborn lock open, a shadow fell over me, blocking out the sun.

I froze. A shiver rippled down my spine, and for a second, I thought it was Corey back on his usual controlling, unannounced bullshit. But when I turned, the air got snatched straight outta my lungs.

It wasn't Corey.

It was him. Legend Boyd. He damn near had my knees buckling just standing there. He looked like a whole dream wrapped in danger. Standing at 6'1", his gym-honed frame filled out his white t-shirt with his tight muscles budging. His smooth dark-chocolate skin glowed against the sunlight, and his face... Lord. Sharp jawline, high cheekbones, and a scar near his jaw that whispered of past fights and hard-earned victories. His eyes, though, stopped me dead. Deep and piercing, like they could see right through me, and maybe they could. Those were eyes that had seen pain, made hard choices, but still held secrets he wasn't giving up easy.

His fresh waves were spinning, glinting like black satin under the sunlight, and that platinum Jesus piece resting on his chest looked expensive and real, not that fake, green-turning mess Corey used to flaunt. Even his designer sneakers were spotless, and the way he carried himself. Spoke of straight dominant power. The kind that made other niggas look away when he walked past and had women holding their breath, hoping for a glance.

"Hey," he said, his deep voice rubbed against my spine giving me all kinds of bad intentions. *"I ain't mean to spook you."*

I felt heat creeping up my neck, my body suddenly very aware of how close he was standing to me.

"Get it together, Dee," I scolded myself. *"He's just a guy. A fine ass, probably got bodies under his belt, and could ruin my life in the best way type of guy."*

"No worries," I replied, trying to play it cool. "I was just... beefing with this mailbox." I gestured with my hand in the direction of the mailboxes, my bracelets jingling as my hands fidgeted nervously.

Legend's lips curved into a smile that had my coochie doing cartwheels. "Down girl," I hissed.

"The box put up that much fight?" He asked, his platinum grill flashing as he grinned down at me.

"I barely escaped with my life," I joked back, surprising myself with how natural it felt. It's been so long since I actually flirted instead of arguing with Corey over side chicks. I barely know what to say in the presence of this fine ass man.

"We can't have that. Do I need to handle that for you, get it's mind right?" He joked.

I found myself smiling despite my worries, my lips curving up at his intensity. "You're a smooth talker, much better than Corey," I teased lightly, and Legend's eyebrow shot up, the dangerous glint in his brown eyes flashing.

"Corey?" He flexed his tatted arms, his platinum watch gleaming in the sunlight. "That lame ass nigga I done seen making scenes over here. Acting like he somebody important when everybody knows he ain't bout that life?" Legend's deep voice dripped with contempt. "I heard through the streets how he stays playing hoe games. Let me guess, is he the reason for the shadows I been seeing in your eyes?"

"Yeah," I shifted my weight from foot to foot, crossing my thick thighs as I leaned against the mailbox. Ain't no sense lying about facts. "I got five years of dead weight. But I'm trying to drop it now. Nah, I have dropped it. I'm just... tryna find my feet in the aftermath." My voice carried hints of pain I couldn't quite hide.

Legend stepped closer, the subtle mix of his cologne and raw masculinity making my head swim.

"Shit, five years? Shorty, that's a long time to waste on a fuck nigga who ain't worth your time. How you holding up?" His genuine concern for me caught my attention as he spoke, and the sight of his muscles flexing under his t-shirt caused my kitty to thump unconsciously.

My chest tightened. Looking at this fine specimen of a man, all 6'1" of his hood royalty, had me questioning everything. After five years of feeling small next to Corey's basic self, here was somebody looking at me like I was a queen.

A RATCHET CITY GOON'S THANKSGIVING CELEBRATION

"*I can't even front like I'm okay,*" I admitted, my long curls falling forward as I shook my head. "*Being with the wrong nigga for so long... that shit does something to your soul. It had me thinking I ain't deserve better.*" I glanced up at him through my lashes. "*But I'm learning to make better choices.*"

Legend's brown eyes darkened. "*Baby girl, I'd be honored to be one of those better choices,*" he rumbled, that voice hitting places Corey's hoe ass never reached. "*If you're ready to see how a real man handles his business, that is.*"

"*Do you always come at females this hard?*" I laughed, but my body was already singing yes.

"*Nah,*" he stepped even closer, that dangerous energy wrapping around me. "*Only when I see something special. And you got a glow about you, despite what that clown tried to dim.*"

I studied him, with his broad shoulders and perfectly trimmed mustache and goatee. The way other niggas walking by gave him a nod of respect. My fears were still there, but something about Legend made me want to risk it all. Maybe it was the street wisdom in his eyes, or how he looked at me like I was the baddest thing he'd seen.

"*I think, Mr. Legend,*" I said, adjusting my crop top over my curves, "*that I might need to see what kind of upgrade you offering.*"

"*Good. 'Cause since God has put a queen in my path, I ain't the type to let her slip away.*" His smile was deadly beautiful, like a bad boy deciding to play nice.

We shared a laugh that felt like forever, the project buildings around us fading into background noise. The kids playing nearby, the smell of dinner cooking, the sound of distant music playing, it all became the perfect backdrop for this moment.

"*You know what they say about me in these streets?*" Legend asked suddenly, his voice low.

"*That you're' dangerous,*" I replied honestly. "*That you ain't nobody to play with.*"

"*All facts,*" he nodded. "*But for the right one, I can be gentle too. The only question is are you ready to find out which side of me you'll bring out?*"

For the first time since leaving Corey, I felt a slight stirring in my chest. Not just hope, but possibility. Like maybe God was finally blessing me with the kind of love I can put my trust in.

The sun hit Legend's face just right, making that dangerous gleam in his eyes look even more intense. I caught myself staring at how his muscles moved under his white tee, thinking 'bout how different he was from Corey's string bean build.

"*You studying me pretty hard, ma,*" Legend teased, his grill flashing as he smirked. "*See something you like?*"

"*Maybe,*" I shot back, my body swaying slightly as I adjusted my stance. "*But I ain't trying to boost your ego too quick. Might have you thinking you got me sprung already.*"

"*Too late for that. Been watching you move through these projects for a minute. The way you carry yourself... it's different from these other females out here.*" He chuckled low, the sound rumbling through the space between us.

"*Oh really?*" I raised an eyebrow, my heart beating fast. "*What you been seeing then, since you been watching so hard?*"

"*I seen a queen trying to play small for a peasant. I seen you walking these blocks looking sad when you should've been shining. It made me wanna pull up on Corey more than once.*" Legend's eyes traveled over me slow, like he was memorizing every curve.

"*Why didn't you?*" I asked, genuinely curious.

"*Because,*" he stepped closer, close enough I could smell the way his cologne mixed with his natural scent, "*as a female you gotta figure out your worth on your own. Can't no man show you what you refuse to see for yourself. So, I waited.*"

"*Damn,*" I whispered, my face heating up under his intense gaze. "*You different for real. I ain't used to nobody talking to me with this much real in their voice.*"

"*Get used to it,*" he reached out, his finger barely brushing my chin, that small touch sent electricity through my whole body. "*I ain't the type to play games or tell sweet lies. These streets have taught me life is too short for that fake shit.*"

The projects was still alive around us. I could hear somebody's car stereo thumping, kids laughing, different music floating past with the Allen Avenue traffic, but it all felt distant. It was like me and Legend was in our own world.

"*You're scary though,*" I admitted, looking up at his towering frame. "*Not because I think you'd hurt me, but... everything about you screams real. And after living with fake so long...*"

A RATCHET CITY GOON'S THANKSGIVING CELEBRATION

"*Being real is all I got, shorty. These streets know my name for a reason. But the heart beating under all this,*" he gestured to himself, "*that's something special I only show to the one who deserves it.*" Legend's face softened just a fraction, but his eyes stayed intense.

A cool breeze swept through the projects, making me shiver slightly. Legend noticed immediately, his sharp eyes missing nothing.

"*Cold, ma?*" Without waiting for an answer, he stepped closer, his broad frame blocking the wind naturally. "*Maybe we should take this conversation somewhere warmer than these mailboxes.*"

My stomach fluttered, my thighs pressing together unconsciously. "*You moving kind of fast, big head,*" I teased, but my body was already leaning toward him.

Legend's laugh was deep and dangerous in all the right ways. "*Nah baby, ain't nothing about me moving fast. When I see something I want, I take my time. Make sure I do it right.*" His platinum grill caught the light as he smiled. "*I was thinking maybe we could go grab some food from 'Orlandeaux's Café' out on the lake. Their yams almost as sweet as that smile you been trying not to give me.*"

"*You trying to take me on a real date? In these streets where everybody can see?*" My heart kicked up a notch, remembering how Corey never wanted to take me out in public.

"*Shit yeah,*" Legend's eyes darkened with intensity. "*I want everybody to see what I'm working with. Let these niggas know you got somebody solid behind you now,*" his strong tatted arms flexed. "*Unless you ain't ready for that kind of attention...*"

"*The kind of attention where other females gonna be mad jealous seeing me with the legendary Legend Boyd?*" I smirked, my wide hips shifting as I adjusted my stance. "*Or the kind where niggas gonna know I'm off limits?*"

"*Both,*" he stepped even closer, that dangerous energy making my skin tingle. "*Cause once I claim something, these streets know I don't play about what's mine.*"

The way he said '*mine*' had parts of me throbbing I forgot existed. "*And what makes you think I'm trying to be claimed?*" I challenged, but my body was betraying me, swaying toward him.

"The way your eyes light up when I step to you," Legend's voice dropped lower, just loud enough for me. *"The way you trying not to smile but can't help it. How your body's responding to my energy right now..."*

"Damn," I breathed, my long curls falling back as I looked up at his towering frame. *"You read everybody this well?"*

"Nah ma," his finger traced my jawline so light it felt like cotton. *"Just the ones worth studying. So, what you say? Let me feed you proper, show you how a real one move?"*

There was a prolonged silence between us as I stood there taking him in. Legend was a feast for the eyes and I took my time getting my fill. Corey had nothing on Legend in the looks department, so I was in heaven.

"Damn, ma," his deep voice rumbled, low and deliberate. *"You gon' keep me standin' here all night, or you gon' let me see that smile and take you out?"*

I felt my cheeks burning, a heat I couldn't hide no matter how hard I tried. I turned away, pretending to be indifferent, twirling a curl around my finger like I wasn't hanging on his every word.

"What smile?" I muttered, trying to sound nonchalant. Half of me prayed he didn't hear, but the other half... the other half needed him to.

"That one," he shot back without pause, his voice edged with playful confidence. *"The one you just tried to hide. You can't play me, shorty. Now what's up? We goin' or nah?"*

I glanced up, my curls falling over one shoulder, my lips parting as I tried to play it cool. But the way his presence filled the space between us had me off balance. His eyes dark and intense, like he could see straight through my bravado, locked onto mine, and for a second, I forgot how to breathe.

"Are you sure I'm what you want, Legend?" I blurted out, sharper than I intended. My nerves were on edge, my palms damp with sweat as I tried to steady myself. *"I'm not exactly in the best condition right now. I've been through a lot. I'm not gonna be easy to deal with."*

He stepped closer, his sheer size making me feel like the air got heavier. The scent of his cologne hit me again, bold and masculine with a dangerous hint of spice. It wasn't just a smell; it was a statement. The kind of scent that warned you he wasn't just trouble, he was the trouble your mama prayed you'd never meet.

A RATCHET CITY GOON'S THANKSGIVING CELEBRATION

"*Damn straight, Deandra,*" he murmured, his voice dropping into a tone that made the back of my neck tingle. "*I don't just want you, I see you. I know what I'm gettin', and trust me, ma, I'm good with it.*"

I swallowed hard, my heart racing. He had this way of pulling me in, like I didn't have a choice in the matter. My walls, the ones I tried to quickly construct after leaving Corey and swore no one could ever penetrate again. They began to break, they felt like paper when he looked at me like that.

"Okay, Legend," I whispered, barely able to hear myself. "*I'm trusting you with me. Don't make me regret it. I've had enough regrets to last a lifetime.*"

"*I got you, shorty. That's a promise. Now stop playin' and let's go eat. I don't do well with waitin', especially when it's for somethin' I want,*" he leaned in, his lips curving into a smirk that made me weak.

I didn't argue. My body was already moving on instinct, following him like he'd cast some kind of spell on me. His hand pressed lightly against the small of my back, guiding me toward his Monte Carlo, and I swore I felt that touch all the way down to my toes.

His car was parked in 'The Middle' off by itself like he owned the block, blacked out, clean as hell, with chrome rims that gleamed under the streetlights. It looked as dangerous as Legend himself, and when he opened the door for me, I caught my reflection in the glossy paint. My lips were parted and my breath was coming faster than it should've been.

"*You good?*" he asked, tilting his head as he held the door open. His eyes scanned me, and it wasn't just a look, it was a claim. Like he already knew I was his, even if I hadn't figured it out yet.

"Yeah," I managed to say, clutching the mail in my hands as I slid into the seat. It smelled like leather and him, a heady, intoxicating, and completely overwhelming scent. I was drowning in it, but somehow, I didn't mind.

He swaggered around to the driver's side, folding his large frame into the seat with a fluid ease that didn't match his size. When he turned to me, his grin was back, and it was impossible not to smile back.

"*You ready, ma?*" He asked.

"*Yeah, I'm ready.*" I nodded, my voice catching in my throat.

THE DRIVE TO THE LAKE was short, but it felt like an eternity. The radio played something low and smooth, but all I could focus on was him, the way his hands gripped the wheel, the way his jaw flexed when he caught me sneaking glances. I tried to keep it together, but my thoughts were all over the place. I hadn't been this close to a real man before, not one who looked at me like I was the only thing that mattered.

"So why you lookin' at me like that?" He broke the silence first.

"Like what?" I blinked, caught off guard.

"Like you tryna figure out if I'm too much for you," he said, a teasing edge in his voice. "You ain't gotta overthink it, Deandra. I'm not here to hurt you. I'm here to make you feel somethin' real. Something tangible that you can believe in. I know you've been through a lot and I'm willin' to go slow. Take things at your pace. You're good with me ma, and you can count on that. I'm not going to hurt you."

"What makes you so sure you can do that?" His words hit me harder than I wanted to admit.

"'Cause I know how to take care of what's mine. And you, shorty? You're already mine. You just don't know it yet," he glanced over, his eyes locking onto mine for a second too long.

The restaurant was a small spot by the water, dimly lit with candles flickering on the tables. It was quieter than I expected, but it felt right, intimate, almost like it was just for us. Legend pulled out my chair, his hand brushing against mine, and I felt that same flutter in my stomach.

Dinner was more than food; it was a dance of words and looks, of guarded confessions and unspoken promises. He told me about growing up in Allendale, about how he learned to hustle because the world didn't give him a choice. And I told him about my dreams, the ones I thought I'd have with Corey. But with Legend, it felt safe to hope again.

By the time we finished, I was buzzing, not from alcohol, I didn't have any, but from him. He leaned back in his chair, his gaze smoldering as he watched me.

"You keep lookin' at me like that, shorty, and I might forget my manners."

"Maybe I don't mind." I bit my lip, the heat in his eyes making my skin tingle. Being with Legend made me wanna give him every part of me, a part I never felt comfortable enough to share with Corey.

A RATCHET CITY GOON'S THANKSGIVING CELEBRATION

"Let's get outta here. I got somethin' better to show you," he smirked, standing and offering his hand.

Legend drove us to his one bedroom apartment in Castlewood, tucked off Bert Kouns Industrial Loop. The hum of the engine filled the silence as I stared out the window, my heart pounding against my ribs. I didn't know what to expect, but my body was already betraying me, reacting to the way he carried himself, the confidence, the heat in his gaze, the way he seemed to command every space he entered. When he pulled into the lot, he turned to me, and for a moment, I couldn't look away. His eyes were a dark, smoldering promise, and the way his lips curled into a slow grin sent a rush of warmth to my cheeks and something deeper, a flutter low in my stomach that I couldn't quite explain.

As we stepped into his place, the subtle scent of cedar and leather filled the air, blending perfectly with the faint trace of his cologne. The apartment was simple but clean, with muted tones and an air of quiet strength, just like him. My nerves tangled with anticipation, and every glance, every accidental brush of his hand against mine, heightened the tension swirling between us. When he leaned casually against the counter, his eyes lingering on me as if he could read every thought I tried to suppress, I felt my pulse quicken. There was something about the way he watched me, like he wanted to take his time but didn't plan on letting me leave without knowing exactly what it felt like to be the center of his world, if only for a night.

"You don't gotta be nervous, Dee. We ain't doin' nothin' you ain't ready for," Legend said, his deep voice rumbling low as he leaned back against the counter. His sharp eyes softened as they locked on me, but even with that tenderness, he still looked dangerous, the kind of man you'd think twice about crossing.

Legend's presence felt bigger than the room. He had that untouchable vibe, like a street king who didn't need to say much to command respect. His white tee stretched across his broad shoulders, and his Jesus piece caught the dim light from the lamp in the corner. Tattoos inked his forearms, speaking stories I'd never ask him to tell, and yet, here he was, looking at me with patience I didn't think he had.

He walked over to me, took my hand and led me until we both settled on the leather couch facing each other.

"Okay ma. You're safe with me. What's goin' on?" He brushed a stray hair behind my ear.

I fidgeted with my fingers, my nerves dancing. *"That's not why I'm nervous,"* I mumbled, barely above a whisper. My voice trembled, betraying me, and I hated it.

"Then what's up? Talk to me, ma." He leaned forward, resting his elbows on his knees, his dark eyes narrowing like he was trying to read my thoughts.

"I've never done this before, so I'm nervous... and a little scared," I admitted, my words tumbling out in a rush. The weight of my confession settled heavy in the air.

Legend leaned back, blinking as the words sank in.

"Damn," he said, his voice barely above a murmur. For a moment, the room was silent except for the faint hum of the ceiling fan circulating air through the room.

Heat rushed to my cheeks, and I lowered my gaze, unable to look him in the eye. My mind spiraled, doubts creeping in. *"What if he doesn't want me now? What if I ruin this moment?"*

"Hey, hey, look at me." His voice was firm but gentle, pulling me out of my thoughts. When I lifted my head, his gaze wasn't mocking or impatient, it was steady, grounding me.

"I ain't gon' lie, you caught me off guard with that one. But listen," he said, his voice softening, *"you bein' real with me? That means somethin'. We ain't gotta rush nothin', Dee. I'll move at your pace. I want you comfortable, feel me? This ain't about me, it's about us."*

"It's just... this is a big deal for me. I don't wanna mess it up." I let out a shaky breath, feeling my chest loosen just a bit.

"Mess it up? Girl, you actin' like I'm here for a perfect performance. This ain't a test, Dee. It's us. And I want it to be special for you. You deserve that." Legend smirked, that cocky, lopsided grin that made my stomach flip.

"You make it sound so easy," I whispered. I felt my eyes sting, the rawness of his words catching me off guard.

"It is easy when you got the right one, and I'm tellin' you, you're my right one. Ain't no rush. I'm here for you, however you need." He chuckled, low and raspy, then reached out to take my hand. His touch was warm, his calloused palm wrapping around mine.

I studied his face, the hard lines softened by his sincerity. *"Could I trust him? Could I give him this part of me and not regret it?"*

A RATCHET CITY GOON'S THANKSGIVING CELEBRATION

The room felt safe, even though his apartment screamed danger. The open floor plan, the faint scent of his cologne mixed with the lingering smell of weed, the dark leather furniture, it all mirrored him. Rugged but magnetic. A place where the world couldn't reach me, where he was the protector of this small, raw corner of my life.

"I'm scared," I admitted, my voice breaking slightly.

"I know, Dee. But let me show you that you don't gotta be. It's just me and you tonight. Nobody else, no distractions, no pressure." Legend scooted closer, his knee brushing mine.

I nodded, biting my bottom lip. My heart pounded as his fingers brushed my cheek, tucking another strand of my hair behind my ear. His touch was careful, reverent, like I was something precious. The way his dark eyes studied me made me feel seen in a way I never had before.

"You ever think about what you want? How you want it to feel?" he asked, his voice low, almost a whisper.

"I want to feel... safe," I said. "And wanted. Like this means something."

"It does mean somethin', Dee. To me, too." His lips curved into a soft smile, one that made my breath hitch. "I'm not just here to get at you. I'm here 'cause I see somethin' in you I ain't found anywhere else. You got my heart movin' different, and I don't take that lightly."

Tears pricked at the corners of my eyes again, but this time, they weren't from fear. They were from the overwhelming feeling of being cared for, being valued.

I nodded again, the lump in my throat making it hard to speak. He leaned in slowly, his lips brushing mine in the lightest kiss. It wasn't rushed or greedy. It was tender, and it unraveled the last of my hesitation.

As the night unfolded, Legend kept his promise. Every touch was slow, deliberate. He didn't rush me. He traced his fingers over my skin like he was memorizing every inch, every shiver, every whispered breath. His kisses were deep, unhurried, as if he had all the time in the world to show me I was his focus.

"You good, Dee? You with me?" The room seemed to fade away as we moved together, his words soft in my ear, grounding me.

"I'm with you," I whispered back, my voice steady this time.

And when the moment came, it wasn't scary or rushed. It was sweet, filled with warmth and trust. Legend guided me, his hands never leaving mine, his eyes locked on me like I was the only thing that mattered.

When it was over, he pulled me close, his arm draped protectively over me.

"You good?" he asked again, his voice laced with concern.

"Yeah. I'm good." I nodded, a small smile tugging at my lips.

"You're somethin' else, Dee," he murmured, pressing a kiss to my forehead. *"Ain't nobody gonna take this from us. You're mine now. You always was. I just had to wait for you to be ready."*

For the first time in what felt like forever, I felt safe. Wrapped in Legend's arms, I knew I'd given a piece of myself to someone who would protect it fiercely. And for that, I was grateful.

CHAPTER THREE
UNWANTED DRAMA

The afternoon sun was setting over the apartments in a multitude of orange arrays. It was casting long shadows across the courtyard where I lived and right now the air was thick with tension. With every breath I took I smelt the scent of fried chicken coming from inside our apartment. The food scent mixed with the faint, metallic tang of rust from the old iron gates surrounding the complex. A faint breeze carried the sound of kids playing hopscotch on the sidewalk, their laughter subdued as they glanced nervously toward the storm brewing on my doorstep as Corey Anderson made an absurd spectacle of himself.

He stood outside our door, his posture all wrong, stiff, desperate, and angry. His slim frame looked even smaller now, especially when compared to Legend's broad shoulders and steady presence. Corey looked like a boy playing at being a man, his face twisted into a pitiful mix of rage and pleading. His fists were clenched at his sides, but it wasn't strength or confidence that held them tight. It was panic.

I crossed my arms, leaning against the doorframe, keeping my face as calm as I could. Inside, my emotions twisted in anger, disgust, and maybe a little pity. But mostly, I felt resolve. This was it. The last time I was letting this sorry excuse for a man disrupt my life.

"Dee, you gotta listen to me!" Corey's voice cracked as he shouted. His usual smooth talking façade crumbled completely. *"I'm serious! You can't just throw me away like this!"*

"Throw you away? Corey, you threw yourself away a long time ago. I just hadn't realized it yet." I couldn't stop the bitter laugh that slipped out.

"Man, don't do me like this, Dee. We got history! I've been there for you..." His face contorted, veins popping in his neck as he took a step forward.

"You been there?" I cut him off, my voice sharp. "Corey, you ain't been nothin' but a headache. You complain about everything, but don't fix nothin'. You blame everybody else for why you stuck where you are, but it's your own lazy ass that's holdin' you back. And as for me? You've done nothing but drag me down."

His hand shot out and grabbed my arm, the force of his grip making me flinch. For a moment, I could feel the weight of his anger pressing on me, trying to pull me back into the cycle I had finally escaped. But that flinch wasn't fear, it was reflex. I wasn't scared of Corey. Not now, not ever.

"Let. Me. Go." My voice was cold and steady, each word measured and deliberate.

"Dee, I didn't mean..." Corey hesitated, his eyes flickering with uncertainty before his grip loosened.

"Don't." I yanked my arm free, stepping back into the doorway, keeping the barrier between us clear. "I'm done listening to your excuses, Corey. 'I didn't mean to cheat.' 'It ain't my fault she came on to me.' 'If you just gave me one more chance, I'll never do it again.' That's all you ever say, and I'm sick of it. You only come around when you need somethin', money, a favor, somebody to fix your shit. You ain't here for me. You never were."

His mouth opened, but no words came out. For once, he didn't have a slick comeback or a half-assed apology ready. I could see it in his eyes, he knew I was right.

"Dee, come on," he finally said, his voice quieter, almost pleading. "You know I love you."

"You don't love me, Corey. You love what I can do for you. You love havin' somebody to clean up after you, to make you feel like a man when you ain't even close." I shook my head, and a sad smile tugged at my lips.

"What, you think you better than me now? Just 'cause you been runnin' 'round with that nigga Legend?" Corey's face twisted again, anger flaring in his eyes.

"You're damn right I'm better off without you cheating on me all the time. Legend treats me like I matter. He listens to me, supports me, and don't make me feel like I'm carryin' the weight of two people by myself. He's a real man, Corey. Not one that's out here up in every hoe's face that crosses his path. Somethin' you wouldn't understand." I stepped forward, closing the distance between us just

A RATCHET CITY GOON'S THANKSGIVING CELEBRATION

enough to look him dead in the eye. *"So, hell yeah. You're damned right. I'm much better off without you."*

The mention of Legend's name hit Corey hard. I could see it in the way his shoulders slumped, the fire in his eyes dimming. Legend's shadow loomed over Corey even when he wasn't here, his strength, his confidence, the way he made me feel like I was worth something.

"Dee, I can change," Corey said, his voice cracking again. *"I can be what you need."*

"Nah, Corey. You had your chances. You wasted 'em all. Now it's time for me to move on." I shook my head slowly, stepping back toward the door.

Corey reached out and grabbed my arm again. This time in a punishing grip. I glanced over my shoulder looking him dead in the eye.

"Let me go, Corey," I sighed, my voice steady, my heart calm, but my patience long gone.

If there was ever a sign that things were done in a relationship, it's when a woman feels absolutely nothing for the nigga. No love, no hate, no lingering hope. Looking at Corey now, all I felt was pure, unfiltered disgust.

My mind raced even as my heart stayed still.

"How did I ever let this fool have so much control over me? How did I sit through his lies, his cheating, his gaslighting?" Those days were over. Corey didn't own me anymore, and I was damn sure gonna remind him of that.

"Look, Corey, we're done. You made your choice, and now I've finally made mine. I've moved on, and I suggest you do the same." I pulled my arm back slowly, but his grip tightened like he was clinging to whatever control he thought he still had over me.

"Choice? What fucking choice?" His voice rose, cracking with desperation. *"You can't possibly believe this is what I wanted! You think I don't know I messed up? But you belong to me, Dee. We've been together too long for you to just up and walk away!"*

The audacity of this nigga made me pause, disbelief flickering in my chest. Then, the disgust returned, hotter this time, boiling just beneath my calm exterior. With one hard yank, I tore my arm free from his grip.

"Nigga, you must be out yo' damn mind," I snapped, stepping back and squaring my shoulders. *"You did make a choice, Corey. Every damn time you lied to my face. Every time you stepped out with Teresa, Cynthia, Daisy, or whatever*

other raggedy hoe you slid into bed with. You made your choice. And now I'm making mine."

Corey froze, his mouth opening and closing like he couldn't process what I was saying. He wasn't used to this side of me, the side that didn't bend, didn't forgive, didn't give a fuck.

"*I belong to myself, Corey,*" I continued, my voice rising with each word. "*You don't own me. You never did. And I'm done being your fool. I'm done with the lying, the cheating, the blaming, and the bullshit. Run back to one of your hoes, 'cause this is it. I'm done.*"

The courtyard seemed to still, the fading sunlight casting long shadows across us. Even the kids who'd been playing hopscotch earlier had gone quiet, sensing the tension in the air about to break.

Corey's eyes narrowed, his nostrils flaring. He wasn't used to me standing up to him, and it showed. For years, I'd let him talk circles around me, make me doubt myself, make me feel like I was the problem. But not anymore.

"*Oh, so now you think you're better than me, huh?*" he sneered, his voice low and venomous. "*What, 'cause you got some other hood nigga sniffin' around you? You think Legend cares about you like I do?*"

The mockery in his tone hit a nerve, but I refused to let it show. Corey's jealousy was like a neon sign flashing in front of me. For years, I hadn't seen it for what it was. The way he'd put me down, tried to control me, made me feel small, it was all because he couldn't handle the fact that I didn't need him as much as he needed me. Corey wasn't just a liar and a cheater. He was an abuser. He'd abused my trust, my loyalty, my forgiveness. And now he was mad because I wasn't playing his game anymore.

"*You really got me twisted, Corey,*" I said, my voice cutting through the thick silence between us. "*You don't care about me. You never did. You cared about what I could do for you. How I made you feel like a man when you ain't even close to bein' one. You used me. You played me. But that shit's over.*"

Corey stepped closer, his jaw tight, but before he could spit out whatever bullshit he had lined up, a deep, steady voice cut through the air like a blade.

"*Careful how you talk to my woman.*"

The sound of Legend's voice sent a shiver down my spine, not from fear, but from the raw power it carried. He stepped out of the shadows, his tall frame taking up all the space in the courtyard. His dark hoodie hugged his broad shoulders, and the heavy chain around his neck caught the last rays of sunlight. Everything about him screamed danger, the kind of danger that made people think twice about crossing him.

Legend's gaze locked on Corey, cold and unyielding. His sharp jaw was set, and his lips curved into the slightest smirk, like he was daring Corey to say something stupid. But it wasn't just his presence that made the air shift, it was the way he looked at me, like I was something worth protecting. Something worth fighting for.

"This between me and Dee. Ain't got nothin' to do with you." Corey spoke cautiously as he turned to face him, his bravado faltering for a split second before he puffed out his chest.

"It's got everything to do with me when you can't keep your hands to yourself. Now, I suggest you take a step back before I make you." Legend took a slow, deliberate step forward, his voice low and calm, but laced with menace.

The tension crackled like electricity. Corey's eyes darted between me and Legend, his guts shrinking by the second. He tried to play it cool, but we both knew he was out of his league.

"Corey, just go," I said, my voice firm. "We're done. You don't get to control me anymore. You don't get to hurt me anymore."

Corey just stood there looking stupid, so Legend came forward. Everyone held their breath as he strode further into the courtyard, his tall frame moving with a lethal, predatory grace. The late afternoon light bounced off his dark skin, highlighting the sharp lines of his jaw and the intensity in his dark brown eyes. His clenched fists and the taut muscles in his forearms sent a silent warning to anyone foolish enough to step in his path. He didn't need to say a word, his very presence demanded respect. The crowd instinctively parted, giving him room. Even the kids who had been playing on the sidewalk stopped, their game forgotten as they stared.

"Oh, so you're the new man, huh? Funny how she moved on so fast," Corey sneered, his lips curling in a weak attempt at boasting. "We've only been apart a couple of days, and she's already on to the next."

The crowd murmured, the tension in the air thick. Most of the bystanders exchanged looks of disbelief, their whispers cutting through Corey's weak attempt at bluffing.

"*She ain't cheatin', Nigga!*" Linda 'Lil Goat' Bryant switched forward, her hips swaying sinuously from side to side, every step dripping with confidence and hypnotic. She stopped just short of Corey, her hand perched on her hip. Linda was one of those neighborhood queens who carried herself like royalty, and everyone knew better than to test her. When she walked she turned heads and captured attention. Many men have fucked up their happy homes transfixed by that walk. Her voice dripped with disdain as she addressed Corey. "*You the one been cheatin' for years. Leave that girl alone. It's 'bout time she dropped your hoe ass!*"

"*Boy, gone on 'bout your business. You ain't never deserved her anyway!*" A young woman holding a baby on her hip chimed in from the side, her tone sharp and cutting. The crowd muttered in agreement, and more voices joined in.

"*You been playin' her for years, Corey. You mad 'cause she finally peeped game?*"

"*Leave Dee alone! She's too good for your sorry ass!*"

Corey's face flushed a deep red as the voices stacked against him. He glanced around, clearly rattled by the crowd turning on him. But instead of backing down, his embarrassment morphed into anger. He turned his attention back to Legend, his voice trembling but still filled with false fearlessness.

"*You think you're better than me? You think you can just swoop in and take what's mine?*" He took a shaky step toward Legend, trying to puff up his chest, but the fear in his eyes betrayed him.

Legend didn't move at first, letting the weight of Corey's words hang in the air. Then, slowly, a cold, dangerous smile curved his lips. When he spoke, his voice was calm, even, but there was an edge to it, a quiet menace that made the hairs on the back of my neck stand up.

"*Nah, Nigga,*" Legend said, his tone smooth yet deadly. "*I don't waste my time worryin' 'bout bein' better than the next man. I'm solid in who I am. Confident in the skin I'm in. But you?*" He chuckled, a deep, menacing sound that sent a shiver through the crowd. "*You knew five years ago Dee was too good for you. That's why you spent all this time tryin' to break her down, convince yourself she wasn't. But where you fucked up was thinkin' she'd never wise up to your bullshit. She finally proved you wrong, and now you lookin' stupid out here.*"

A RATCHET CITY GOON'S THANKSGIVING CELEBRATION

Corey opened his mouth to respond, but Legend wasn't finished. He took a slow step closer, his broad shoulders blocking out the sun as he towered over Corey.

"*And another thing,*" Legend said, his voice dropping lower. "*Dee ain't yours. She's mine. And unlike you, I don't just talk about what I'm gon' do, I back it up. So, here's your only warning, back the fuck off before I make you regret ever breathin' in her direction.*"

Corey's bravado crumbled completely. His lips parted, but no words came out. The fear in his eyes was palpable, and he took an involuntary step back. But then, out of desperation or stupidity, he lunged forward, swinging wildly.

Legend didn't flinch. He ducked under the punch with ease, moving so quickly it was like Corey was in slow motion. The counterpunch came fast and hard, a clean hook to Corey's jaw that echoed through the courtyard. Corey stumbled back, clutching his face as gasps and shouts erupted from the crowd.

"*Damn! Did you see that?*"

"*Legend ain't playin'!*"

Corey staggered, trying to regain his footing, but Legend wasn't giving him the chance. When Corey threw another punch, Legend caught his wrist with one hand and twisted it sharply. Corey yelped in pain as Legend shoved him against the iron gate. The metal rattled loudly, and Corey's wide eyes darted around, searching for help that wasn't coming.

"*You done?*" Legend asked, his voice calm but laced with a chilling edge.

"*Legend, stop!*" I shouted, pushing through the crowd. My voice trembled, not with fear for Corey, but fear that Legend might go too far. Corey wasn't worth it.

But Legend wasn't finished. He landed another punch, this one a sharp jab to Corey's gut that made him double over, gasping for air. The crowd erupted again, phones snapping up to record the scene.

"*Got damn! Corey lookin' real bad out here!*"

"*That nigga shoulda stayed at home.*"

Corey crumpled to the ground, blood trickling from his split lip as he wheezed for breath. Legend stood over him, his fists still clenched, murder in his eyes. His chest heaved, and for a moment, it looked like he might strike again.

"*Legend, stop!*" I shouted, grabbing his arm. "*Please. He ain't worth it.*"

Legend's gaze snapped to me, his eyes softening slightly. He stood still for a moment, his jaw clenched, the raw anger in his expression slowly melting into something calmer. With a deep breath, he stepped back, letting Corey collapse fully onto the pavement.

Mr. West and Mr. Wade rushed over to Legend. Both older men carried the kind of no nonsense energy only years of hard work and raising kids in a neighborhood like ours could give. Mr. West, Johnya's father, and Mr. Wade, Deana's father, had been around since I was a kid, always keeping an eye out for trouble. Today was no different.

Both men wore work boots scuffed from years of labor and paint-splattered jeans that spoke of long shifts and honest work. They pushed through the lingering crowd, stepping into the chaos as Legend loomed over Corey's crumpled form, his chest heaving, fists clenched, and murder still dancing in his eyes.

"Whoa, man, that's enough!" Mr. West said, grabbing at Legend's arm. He strained to hold him back, his voice firm but not unkind. *"You made your point. Don't make it worse."*

"C'mon now, young blood," Mr. Wade added, gripping Legend's broad shoulder. His tone carried a warning. *"Don't kill him. He ain't worth it, son."*

Legend's muscles were tight, his body wound like a spring, but he shrugged them off with surprising restraint. He stayed rooted where he was, his sharp jaw clenched, his piercing eyes locked on Corey, who groaned on the pavement like the pathetic coward he was.

"You ever touch her again," Legend growled, his voice low and dangerous, *"and I swear I'll make you regret your mother didn't swallow your bitch ass."*

The crowd gasped, a mix of disbelief and awe at the sheer weight of Legend's words. Even Mr. West and Mr. Wade exchanged glances, their grips loosening as they realized Legend wasn't a man who lost control, he was a man who calculated every move.

Corey, still clutching his side, managed a weak, bitter laugh. Blood smeared his lip as he spit onto the concrete.

"Guess she's got you fooled, huh?" His voice shook as he tried to muster whatever pride he had left. *"You think she's innocent, but she's been with me for five years. It ain't no way she didn't cheat on me with you. Especially seeing how y'all got together so quick."*

A RATCHET CITY GOON'S THANKSGIVING CELEBRATION

His words hit me like a slap, not because they were true, but because I'd allowed this manipulative clown to hold that kind of power over me for so long. My hands clenched into fists at my sides, and my voice came out sharp, trembling with anger.

"*You got no right to talk about loyalty, Nigga,*" I snapped, stepping forward. "*We both know I should've dropped your sorry ass the first time I caught you cheating, when I was twelve! But no, I was stupid. I gave you chance after chance, and you through every single one of 'em away.*"

The crowd murmured in agreement, but it was Legend who silenced Corey completely.

"*Corey,*" Legend said, his voice quiet but cold. "*We both know Dee never cheated on you. Hell, she's never even been with you.*" His lips curved into a dangerous smirk as he leaned in closer to Corey, his towering frame making him look even smaller. "*That pleasure? That was all mine.*"

I felt heat rush to my face as Legend glanced at me, his smirk softening into something more intimate. My head ducked shyly, but the memory of our first night together, the night he made me feel like I was worth something, like I mattered, burned bright in my mind. The pain, the pleasure, the way he held me after... It was a moment Corey could never taint.

Corey's face twisted with rage and disbelief as he pieced together Legend's words. He shot me a look like I'd betrayed him, but the truth was, I owed him nothing. He didn't deserve my loyalty or my guilt.

"*You need to get gone, Corey,*" Mr. West said firmly, stepping between Legend and Corey to block whatever fight was left in him. "*You already embarrassed yourself enough out here.*"

"*Yeah, you lookin' real pathetic, boy,*" Mr. Wade added, shaking his head. "*Take the L and go. Don't make it worse.*"

Corey's eyes darted to the crowd, where murmurs of disapproval and outright laughter greeted him. More voices chimed in, cutting through the tension.

"*Leave her alone!*"

"*You lost, Nigga! Ain't no comin' back from that.*"

"*Stop embarrassing yourself!*"

Legend took another step closer, his towering frame looming over Corey like a shadow. His fists were no longer clenched, but the menace in his posture made it clear he didn't need them. His presence alone was enough to send Corey running.

"*Get the fuck outta here, Corey,*" Legend said, his voice deadly calm. "*And don't let me catch you 'round here again. Dee is mine now. She's no longer any of your concern. Understand?*"

Corey's eyes flicked between me and Legend, his anger melting into humiliation. Finally, he staggered to his feet, brushing off his jeans as if it would somehow salvage his dignity. He stumbled away, shoulders hunched, mumbling curses under his breath.

The crowd began to disperse, murmuring and shaking their heads. Phones slid back into pockets as people whispered about the drama they'd just witnessed.

As the courtyard quieted, Mr. West and Mr. Wade turned to Legend.

"*You good, son?*" Mr. West asked, his voice less stern now. "*It ain't no need for you to be letting a fool like that get under your skin.*"

"*I appreciate y'all steppin' in,*" he said, his voice steady. "*I wasn't tryna take it too far, but sometimes niggas like him need to feel it to understand it.*" Legend nodded, his breathing still heavy, but his fists relaxed at his sides. "*Let's just hope he stays away from Dee.*"

"*True enough,*" Mr. Wade said with a chuckle, clapping Legend on the shoulder. "*Just don't let him drag you down. You got somethin' good here with Dee. Don't let her get caught up in no nonsense.*"

"*I won't,*" Legend promised, his eyes flicking to me. "*She's way too important to me for that.*"

"*Good man,*" Mr. West said, tipping his head before turning to me. "*You okay, Dee?*"

"*I'm fine,*" I said, my voice trembling slightly. "*Thank you both for stepping in.*"

"*Anytime, baby girl,*" Mr. Wade said warmly. "*You deserve better than that fool anyway. Glad you finally realized it.*"

When they left, I turned to Legend. His intense gaze softened as he stepped closer, gently taking me in his arms.

"*You okay?*" he asked, his deep voice rough but full of concern.

"*Yeah. Thanks to you.*" I nodded, tears pricking at the corners of my eyes.

A RATCHET CITY GOON'S THANKSGIVING CELEBRATION

"Ain't nobody gon' hurt you again, Dee. I promise you that." Legend cupped my face, his thumb brushing against my cheek.

And in that moment, as I stood in the fading sunlight with Legend's strong arms wrapped around me, I felt something I hadn't felt in years, safe. Truly, deeply, unshakably safe.

CHAPTER FOUR
LEGEND'S FALL

The sun dipped below the horizon, casting the Jackson Heights Projects in shadows. The dim orange glow over the rust stained brick buildings faded to deep purple, and the cool evening air carried a heavy silence that felt out of place in the usually lively streets. Cracked asphalt littered with debris from the day, broken glass, fast food wrappers, and stray pieces of paper, set the scene for the tension simmering in the air.

I stood in my doorway, one hand gripping the frame while my eyes locked on the outer edge of the adjacent building. That's where Legend stood, facing King Michael. The notorious leader of the Lakeside crew commanded respect just by existing. He was tall and broad shouldered, with a dark expression that seemed carved from stone. His clenched jaw and the subtle narrowing of his eyes said everything he wasn't saying out loud.

Legend stood before him like he wasn't fazed, his posture loose but deliberate, a predator sizing up another alpha. The air around him felt charged, like electricity waiting to strike. He wore a black hoodie that hung just right over his muscular frame, his jeans low slung but clean, and his Timberlands scuffed in a way that made them look purposeful, like they'd been through the kind of battles most wouldn't survive. Everything about him screamed danger, the kind that made people clear a path without him asking.

But this wasn't just some street flex. This was serious, and I knew it. My heart thudded painfully in my chest, each beat heavier than the last as I stared at Legend. I couldn't hear what he was saying to King Michael, but his gestures were calm, controlled, even as the weight of the situation bore down on him.

This is my fault, I thought, my stomach twisting into knots. If I'd just handled Corey myself, if I hadn't needed Legend to step in... maybe he wouldn't be here right now, standing in front of the most dangerous man in the neighborhood, explaining himself.

I bit my bottom lip, my mind racing. *"What if this costs him his spot with the crew? What if Michael decides Legend's actions brought too much heat?"* I'd heard the stories, what happened to people who crossed King Michael or made him look bad. People didn't just lose positions in the crew; sometimes, they disappeared altogether.

I glanced back toward the apartment, wishing I could disappear into the safety of its four walls, but my legs wouldn't move. Instead, I stayed rooted in place, watching the scene unfold. My nails dug into the iron of the doorframe, the chipped paint rough beneath my fingertips. My emotions churned, a mix of guilt, fear, and something deeper I didn't want to name. He didn't deserve to be out there cleaning up my mess.

I shook my head, trying to steady my thoughts. This ain't all on me. Corey pushed me for too long, and Legend stepped up because that's who he is. A real one. A protector. But still... if something happens because of this...

My gaze flicked to Legend again, his broad shoulders framed by the streetlights behind him. He stood tall, his head slightly tilted as he spoke to King Michael. His voice was too low for me to hear, but the tone carried authority, not submission. Even in the face of someone like Michael, Legend didn't back down.

And that's what scared me the most. His confidence, his fearlessness, they were part of why I fell for him, but in moments like this, they felt like a double edged sword.

I wrapped my arms around myself, trying to keep my hands from trembling. My mind wandered to the fight with Corey earlier, the way Legend had stepped in without hesitation. The memory of his fists connecting with Corey's jaw, the cold fury in his eyes as he told Corey to stay away from me, it was raw, brutal, and terrifyingly beautiful. No one had ever stood up for me like that before. But now, it felt like the price of that protection was too high.

"What if he doesn't come back to me tonight? What if this loyalty to me costs him everything he's built?"

My stomach twisted again, and I swallowed hard, forcing myself to focus on the present. King Michael crossed his arms, his dark eyes narrowing slightly as he listened to Legend. Michael's crew stood nearby, their faces unreadable, but their postures tense. No one dared interrupt.

Legend shifted his weight slightly, his hands relaxed at his sides, but his presence was anything but. He radiated a quiet intensity, like a storm ready to break. He wasn't just dangerous, he was deliberate, calculating. Every move, every word was measured, and that's what made him so magnetic. He wasn't just another hood nigga trying to survive; he was a man who thrived under pressure, who turned the streets into his playground and played by his own rules.

As the silence stretched, my chest tightened. I couldn't take it anymore. I had to do something, say something, but what? This wasn't my world. I didn't know the politics, the rules, the unspoken codes that dictated how men like Legend and Michael operated. All I knew was that Legend had put himself on the line for me, and I couldn't let him carry that weight alone.

"Dee." A voice behind me broke through my thoughts. I turned to see Linda 'Lil Goat' Bryant standing there, her face filled with concern. *"You okay?"*

I nodded quickly, though it was a lie. *"I'm fine,"* I said, my voice barely above a whisper.

"You don't look fine," she said, switching closer her hips mesmerizing as they swayed from side to side. Her gaze shifted to Legend and King Michael, and she let out a low whistle. *"Damn. He really out here standin' toe-to-toe with Michael. That's your Goon for real."*

"Yeah... that's him." I couldn't help the small, shaky smile that tugged at my lips.

"Well don't let the bullshit around here fuck wit' what y'all are building. There are gonna be plenty of hoes out here tryna take your spot. Stand firm and you'll be good. You got a real one, hold your head high like you know it."

"Alright, Lil Goat. I appreciate it." I nodded.

"Anytime. Now let me get out of here. I gotta go chase this paper." She waved and ducked around the side of the building, hips swaying side to side putting all of King Michael's crew in a trance.

A RATCHET CITY GOON'S THANKSGIVING CELEBRATION

KING MICHAEL SHOOK his head slowly, his broad shoulders rising and falling with a heavy sigh. Disappointment etched deep lines across his dark face, and the weight of his disapproval hit me harder than any punch I'd ever taken.

"Legend, man," he began, his deep voice vibrating through the thick evening air. The sound carried a quiet authority, the kind that made people stand still and listen. *"I'm tired of cleanin' up messes, you understand. You beat that boy Corey damn near to death in broad daylight. In front of the whole damn projects."*

My jaw tightened, but I kept my posture loose, my hood pulled low over my face to hide the storm brewing in my eyes.

"Corey disrespected my woman, Mike. He put his hands on her. I couldn't let that shit slide." I shifted my weight, my fists still raw and aching from earlier.

Michael's eyes narrowed, and he shook his head again, slower this time, like he couldn't believe what he was hearing.

"I get that. I do. And I would never tell you not to defend your lady. But there are ways to handle that kinda thing, and makin' a damn scene like you did ain't one of 'em," he hissed.

"You know what happens when shit like this goes down. People all over the complex got cell phones, Legend. Videos of you stompin' that nigga are already floatin' around. How the fuck you posed to handle business with all that noise circling you? You done made the spot hot, and now we got a problem." His voice dropped lower, his tone growing sharper, more pointed.

I clenched my fists at my sides, trying to keep my face neutral, but his words were hitting me where it hurt. His words were true. The crowd from earlier had scattered, but the damage was done. Whispers were spreading like wildfire through the projects, and it wouldn't take long for those whispers to reach the wrong ears, cops, rivals, whoever was looking for a reason to come sniffing around.

Michael exhaled sharply, dragging a hand down his face as if trying to compose himself.

"You know how this works, Legend. Heat on you is heat on us. You bring that shit to the set, and it puts everybody at risk. The cops start circlin', lookin' for excuses to shut us down. That's the kinda heat we don't want, we don't need. You feel me?"

I nodded stiffly, the bitter truth settling in my chest. I knew the game. I'd lived it for years. But this wasn't just business, this was Deandra. She wasn't just some girl to me; she was mine. And the thought of Corey putting his hands on her, of him thinking he could get away with it, was enough to set me off all over again.

King Michael's expression was hard, unyielding, but his tone softened slightly, like he was trying to reason with me.

"Look, I know you loyal, and I know you handle your business. That's why I keep you close. You one of my most thorough goons, Legend. But right now? You too hot. Too reckless. You gotta know how to move smarter than this." He stepped closer, his tall frame casting a long shadow under the flickering streetlights.

"Mike, this ain't about me bein' reckless. This about me protectin' what's mine. That nigga Corey put his hands on Deandra. He grabbed her arm hard enough to bruise her, in front of everybody like he ain't got no sense. What was I supposed to do? Let it slide? Pretend like it didn't happen?" I met his gaze, my jaw tightening.

Michael's eyes flicked to me sharply, a flash of understanding passing over his face before his usual mask of control slipped back into place.

"I hear you. And if it was me, I'd wanna handle it the same way. But you ain't just any nigga out here, Legend. You're part of the Lakeside crew. You know what that means, how we gotta move. You make moves like that, it don't just affect you. It puts the whole squad in the line of fire."

I stayed silent, my mind racing as his words sunk in. He wasn't wrong, but that didn't mean I regretted what I did. Corey had it coming, and I'd do it all over again if it meant keeping Deandra safe.

Michael stepped even closer, his voice lowering to almost a growl.

"And let me make somethin' real clear. This ain't about loyalty. I know you loyal. But loyalty don't mean shit if it gets us all taken down. I can't have your drama puttin' us all in danger. So, for right now? You out."

The words hit me like a punch to the gut, but I forced myself to stay composed. I straightened up, meeting Michael's gaze head on.

"You really kickin' me out? Just like that?" I asked.

"Ain't nothin' personal, Legend. You too hot right now. Get yourself together, and maybe we'll talk later. But for now, you out." Michael's expression hardened as he spoke.

"I hear you," I nodded stiffly, my voice tight and my jaw clenched so tight it hurt.

Michael didn't say another word. He turned and walked away, his heavy boots crunching against the gravel as the crew followed him into the shadows.

A RATCHET CITY GOON'S THANKSGIVING CELEBRATION

The air around me felt colder somehow, the weight of disappointment pressing down like a vice on my chest.

As I stood there, alone now, my mind raced. I fucked up. I know I did. But I'd do it again. My fists clenched at my sides as the frustration bubbled up, threatening to spill over. This wasn't just about me losing my spot with the crew. This was about her.

I could still see the fear in Deandra's eyes when Corey grabbed her, the way she flinched, the way her voice shook when she told him to let her go. That image burned into my mind, and no amount of lectures from Michael was gonna make me regret stepping in.

"But now what?" I thought bitterly. Michael's right about one thing, I made the spot hot. Ain't nobody gonna want to do business with me while the cops are sniffing around. *"And what happens if Corey decides to come back?"*

My gaze flicked toward the building where Deandra waited, probably watching everything from the doorway. She didn't ask for this drama, but I'd brought it to her doorstep all the same.

I'll figure it out, I told myself, forcing a deep breath. Ain't nobody takin' what's mine, and I ain't lettin' nobody put her in harm's way again.

With one last glance at the shadows where Michael had disappeared, I turned and started back toward Deandra. She was all that mattered now, and no matter what it cost me, I'd make sure she was safe.

THE AIR WAS STILL THICK with the aftermath of the day, the usual chatter of the block reduced to whispers carried on the cool breeze. I sat on the steps of my building, my knees pulled to my chest, watching Legend approach.

Even in the low light, he moved with a raw, magnetic energy that made him impossible to ignore. His muscles were tense under his hoodie, his jaw set, and his hands flexed at his sides like they weren't quite ready to relax. Every step he took carried a quiet menace, a warning to anyone foolish enough to step in his way. Yet, when his eyes landed on me, they softened just enough to unravel the knot in my chest.

My heart pounded, a mix of fear and guilt clawing at me. When he reached me, I couldn't hold it back anymore.

"I'm so sorry, Legend," I whispered, my voice breaking. *"This... this is all my fault. You got cut from the crew because of me."*

"Dee, don't do that," he said, his voice low and rough, but steady. *"This ain't your fault."* He crouched down in front of me, his large hand reaching up to tuck a stray curl behind my ear. The gesture was so gentle, so at odds with the dangerous aura he carried, it made my chest tighten.

"But it is!" I blurted out, tears pricking at my eyes. *"If I hadn't needed you to step in. If Corey hadn't grabbed me... none of this would've happened. You wouldn't be in this mess."*

Legend sighed, running a hand over his head, his wavy Cesare cut catching the light for just a second. He looked away for a moment, his sharp features hardening, but I knew it wasn't because of me. The frustration was there, but it wasn't directed at me, it was at the situation, at Corey, at the world that was pullin' at him.

"Listen to me," he said, his voice firm but not harsh. *"Corey crossed a line, Dee. The moment he put his hands on you, he made it my business. You're my woman. That means it's my job to protect you, and I'll do it every damn time. All the rest of this bullshit?"* He waved a hand dismissively. *"It's just background noise. Ain't no man gon' touch you and walk away like it's sweet."*

His words touched my soul, but the guilt still clung to me like a second skin. My mind raced with everything that had happened, replaying the way Corey had grabbed me, the way Legend had stepped in without hesitation, and the fallout that followed.

"But you lost your crew, Legend. Michael and the fellas... they looked up to you, relied on you. And now it's gone. Because of me." My voice cracked as I whispered.

Legend tilted my chin up, forcing me to meet his gaze. His dark brown eyes burned with intensity, but there was no anger in them, just conviction.

"Nah, Dee. That's on Corey," he said, his tone fierce. *"He the one who brought this on himself, not you. And yeah, I lost my spot with King Michael. That's just how the game goes sometimes. But don't you ever think this is on you. You hear me?"*

"I just... I hate that you had to choose between keeping your place and protecting me." Tears slipped down my cheeks, and I nodded, even though the guilt hadn't let go yet.

A RATCHET CITY GOON'S THANKSGIVING CELEBRATION

"*There wasn't no choice,*" he said, his voice dropping to a low, steady growl that sent a shiver through me. "*You're more important than any crew, any rank, any reputation. You're worth it, Dee. You're mine. And I'm never lettin' another nigga think he can touch you and get away with it.*"

His words cracked something open inside me. Relief washed over me, but it was tangled with fear, fear that this wasn't over, that Corey or someone else would come back, that Legend would get hurt because of me. The thought terrified me.

"*What if this gets worse?*" I asked, my voice barely above a whisper. "*What if this is just the beginning of more trouble for you?*"

Legend's jaw tightened for a moment, and I could see the flicker of turmoil in his eyes. He was weighing his words, trying to shield me from the doubt he couldn't completely push away. But when he spoke, his voice was steady, filled with quiet determination.

"*We'll figure it out,*" he promised. "*Ain't nothin' in this life easy, Dee. I know that better than most. But I'm not lettin' anything happen to you. You're safe with me. Always.*"

His confidence was reassuring, but I couldn't ignore the weight of his words. I didn't want to be the reason he suffered, the reason he lost more than he already had.

"*I don't want you to suffer because of me, Legend,*" I said, my voice trembling. "*You don't deserve that. I don't deserve you.*"

His hand tightened on mine, and he pulled me closer, his broad frame radiating warmth and strength.

"*Suffering's part of the life I chose,*" he said quietly, his voice low and raw. "*But loving you? That makes it worth it. Protecting you makes it worth it.*"

I buried my face in his chest, breathing in his scent, cologne, sweat, and a faint trace of the fight still clinging to him. His heartbeat was steady under my ear, grounding me in a way nothing else could. For the first time in years, I didn't feel like I was facing my struggles alone.

Legend's thoughts were a storm as he held me. "*This shit's a mess,*" he admitted aloud to himself. "*I'm out the crew, my name too hot, and Michael's pissed. But I'd do it all again. Corey crossed the line, and I wasn't gonna let that slide. I ain't lettin' no man disrespect my woman.*"

He clenched his jaw, the frustration bubbling under the surface, but he pushed it down. He couldn't let it show, not to me. *"Dee don't need to carry that weight. This ain't her fault. This is on me, and I'll handle it. Just like I always do."*

"We're gonna get through this, Dee. Together. I promise you, you ain't carryin' this weight alone." His grip tightened slightly as he pressed a kiss to the top of my head.

His words gave me a sliver of hope, enough to hold onto. But as much as I wanted to believe him, the fear still lurked in the back of my mind, waiting for a chance to prove me right.

CHAPTER FIVE NEW ALLIANCES

The late afternoon sunlight spilled over the Jackson Heights Projects, painting the cracked asphalt and weathered brick buildings in a golden glow. The air was still heavy with the faint hum of distant music and the occasional bark of a dog. I leaned against my chrome black-on-black Monte Carlo, the sun glinting off the polished surface, lost in thought. The ache from my fallout with King Michael still lingered, raw and biting, but I wasn't the type to dwell on the small stuff. This life came with losses, and I knew the game too well to let one setback take me out.

Hustling's in my blood, I reminded myself. It's the only life I know. The gig with King Michael's crew had been smooth, a machine I could run blindfolded. Now that it was gone, I had to switch gears, find another way forward. My mind turned deadly to other possibilities. *"Kickin' in a backdoor or two might be my next move,"* I thought, my jaw tightening. I was too good at this to let the streets forget me.

That's when I spotted them, Stone, Myron, and C-Lo, rolling up on the block. They moved with that quiet authority that only came from running the streets and earning respect. Stone led the way, tall and broad-shouldered, his marble-gray eyes sharp and calculating, scanning every angle like he saw things the rest of us didn't. Myron followed behind closely, built like a light weight boxer, thin and well-muscled, his clean fade and sharp jawline giving him the look of someone you didn't argue with. C-Lo, the last of the trio, had a smooth, almost lazy demeanor, but the menace in his green eyes made it clear that beneath the charm was a man you didn't cross. These weren't just street-level players. These were bosses.

I'd seen them work before, quiet, efficient, ruthless. They didn't waste time on messiness, and their crew ran like a well-oiled machine. If they were here, they had a reason. My instincts sharpened as they approached.

"What's good, Legend?" Stone's deep voice broke the silence first. His tone was calm, but there was an edge to it, like he wasn't just here to shoot the shit. *"We need to have a word if you got a minute. You good to roll with us?"*

"Yeah, I'm down." I nodded slowly, my curiosity piqued.

I climbed into the back of their black SUV, the scent of expensive cologne and faint traces of weed filling the air. The leather seats were soft, but the tension inside was anything but. My instincts told me to stay alert, even as Stone, sitting beside me, radiated a calm confidence that demanded respect.

They didn't say much at first, letting the silence stretch as we rolled through the projects. I leaned back, my hands resting on my thighs, watching the world roll by through the tinted windows. *"They've been watching me,"* I thought, my chest tightening. *"If they're serious, this could be my shot."*

"We've had our eye on you for a minute," Stone said finally, his voice cutting through the quiet. He turned his head slightly, his gray eyes locking onto mine. *"We like how you move. You handle your business quiet and smooth. Ain't too many cats left like that out here."*

"Yeah, man. Most niggas be out here screamin' for attention, makin' noise they don't need. But you? You get shit done without all that flash. That's rare." C-Lo twisted in the front passenger seat to face me, a faint smirk on his lips.

"Even how you handled Corey was solid. Messy, yeah, but solid. That nigga needed to be put in his place, and you made sure he stayed there." Myron, who was driving, glanced at me through the rearview mirror. His steady gaze added weight to their words.

"Appreciate that," I said, keeping my tone steady. *"I just do what needs to be done."* I nodded my head slightly, letting their words sink in.

"We respect that. But we didn't approach you before 'cause you were with King Michael's crew. Out of respect, we didn't want to step on his toes." Stone nodded, a faint smile tugging at the corner of his lips.

"Yeah, I get that." I tensed slightly at the mention of Michael, but I kept my face neutral.

"Michael's not wrong about why he let you go. The Corey situation brought too much heat to the block. You know how it is. Heat makes people nervous, and when

A RATCHET CITY GOON'S THANKSGIVING CELEBRATION

people get nervous, they make mistakes." Stone's tone shifted slightly, growing more serious.

"It ain't about loyalty, man. Michael had to protect the bigger picture. But that don't mean you ain't solid." C-Lo nodded in agreement, his laid-back demeanor hardening just enough to show he was serious.

"The game's about survival, Legend. Michael had to make a move to keep his operation clean. You ain't the first, and you won't be the last to get sacrificed to keep shit movin'. Every nigga in his crew got mouths to feed. It was let go of one to save the many." Myron's voice cut in, calm but direct.

I sat back, absorbing their words. It makes sense, I thought bitterly. Michael's move wasn't personal, it was business. Still, the sting of being cut loose burned in my chest. But I wouldn't let it show. Ain't no room for ego out here.

"Here's the thing, Legend. Now that you're a free agent, we want you on our team. You know how to stay under the radar and still get shit done. That's exactly what we need. I'm offering you a spot as a lieutenant. You'd be running your own territory, managing your own squads. No micromanaging, no bullshit. Just business." Stone leaned forward, his sharp eyes locking onto mine.

I tilted my head slightly, my mind racing. A lieutenant spot wasn't just a job, it was power, responsibility, control. And with Stone's crew? That was a come up.

"You serious about this?" I asked, my tone measured, though my chest tightened with excitement.

"Dead serious," Stone said, his voice low and commanding. "We move different. More organized. No loose ends. We ain't just about makin' money, we're about buildin' somethin' that lasts. And we think you can help us do that."

"You in, or you still cryin' over King Michael?" C-Lo added smirking, crossing his arms.

"Nigga, I ain't cryin' over shit, but I'm in," I barked a short laugh, shaking my head.

The energy in the car shifted immediately. Stone, Myron, and C-Lo nodded, sealing the deal with firm handshakes. This wasn't just another gig. This was an opportunity to rebuild, to rise higher than before.

As the SUV pulled back into the projects, I stepped out, feeling a surge of ambition. Stone clapped me on the back as he passed, his smirk confident.

"Welcome to the squad, Legend. Let's get this money," he nodded.

"Already..." I hit them wit' a head nod as they passed.

I watched them leave, the weight of the day settling over me. *"This is it,"* I thought, a faint smirk tugging at my lips. *"My next move. My chance to build somethin' real."*

I turned back toward my Monte Carlo, the late afternoon sun glinting off the hood, and I felt a spark of determination. The streets ain't seen the last of me yet.

OVER THE NEXT TWO AND a half weeks, I found myself settling into my new position with Stone's organization. The shift in environment was like night and day compared to my time with King Michael's crew. With Stone, Myron, C-Lo, and the rest of the fellas, there was a real sense of camaraderie. Respect wasn't just demanded, it was earned and reciprocated. Trust flowed naturally, and the responsibilities I'd taken on made me feel like more than just another player in the game. I was part of something bigger, something more structured.

The way Stone ran his operation was next level. Everything had a system, a purpose. From the streets to legitimate fronts, he'd built a network that wasn't just about surviving, it was about thriving. That's how I ended up drawing a weekly paycheck from a construction company on paper, making over $75,000 a year. For someone in the life, that kind of setup was unheard of. But Stone wasn't like most bosses. He thought long-term, and he made sure his people ate without catching unnecessary heat.

One day, during a meeting in Stone's warehouse, set up like a lawncare business, we got into the details of my new responsibilities. The place was clean, modern, and sharp, just like him. The dark leather couches, glass coffee table, and floor-to-ceiling windows screamed power from the lounge area of the conference room, but it was the overall vibe in the room that commanded respect. Myron leaned back in his seat at the conference table, sipping on a bottled water, while C-Lo sat with one leg draped casually over the other, his eyes watchful but relaxed. Stone stood at the head of the conference table, his marble-gray eyes fixed on me.

A RATCHET CITY GOON'S THANKSGIVING CELEBRATION

"*Legend,*" Stone started, his voice deep and steady, "*I brought you in because you know how to move. I don't need flashy. I don't need reckless. I need smart. You've proven you got what it takes, but in this organization, every move matters.*"

"I hear you," I said, nodding. "*Ain't no half-steppin' with me. I do what needs to be done.*"

"*That's what I like to hear,*" Stone replied, a faint smirk tugging at the corner of his lips. "*Now, here's what's next. We got a couple of projects that need hands-on oversight. Myron's handling the Eastside developments, and C-Lo's running the logistics for the supply chain. I'm puttin' you on the Westside expansion. You'll be coordinating with the construction crews, keepin' the books clean, and making sure no one's skimming off the top.*"

"*Westside's been tricky lately,*" Myron added, his tone serious. "*A couple of small-time crews been sniffin' around, thinkin' they can make moves. You'll need to keep an eye on 'em.*"

"*If they step outta line, you know what to do. But keep it quiet. We don't need heat right now. If they need to be dealt with, hit up Killian, Kahmala, Steel, Blade, Kilayla, and Khiershan. Keep your hands clean, that's what we got hittas for,*" C-Lo chuckled, his laid-back tone belying the menace in his words.

I nodded, letting their words sink in. This ain't just about muscle, it's about strategy. About thinkin' three moves ahead.

"*You up for it?*" Stone asked, his piercing gaze locked on mine.

"*I'm always up for it. This is what I do.*" I leaned forward slightly, my voice steady.

"*That's what I like to hear. Let's get to work.*" Stone grinned, clapping me on the shoulder.

As much as I was diving headfirst into my new responsibilities, my relationship with Deandra was growing, too. There was something about the way she looked at me now, like I wasn't just a street nigga to her. I was her man, and she was proud of that. Proud of me. And that pride made me want to be better, to give her the life she deserved.

On our first date since everything went down, we hit 'Tinseltown' to catch an action movie. Deandra showed up in a simple pair of jeans and a fitted tee, but she looked so good, I couldn't stop staring. The way she laughed at the funny scenes in the movie had me smiling like a square, her joy was infectious.

"You really out here crackin' up at that weak ass line?" I teased, leaning close as the credits rolled.

"Don't act like you didn't laugh, too. You just tryin' to be cool." She smacked my arm playfully.

"Maybe," I admitted with a smirk, watching the way her eyes lit up. That laugh, that smile, it's worth everything.

The next date, we hit 'Olive Garden', splitting pasta while we talked about everything and nothing. She had this way of making even the simplest conversation feel important.

"I've been thinkin' about goin' to college," she said, her eyes sparkling as she twirled her fork in the fettuccine.

"What you wanna study?" I asked, genuinely curious.

"Business or social work," she replied, her tone confident. "I wanna open my own business one day. Something non-profit and affordable."

"You can do it, Dee. You got the drive. Whatever you need to make it happen, I got you." I leaned back, watching her with a mix of admiration and pride.

"You really mean that?" Her cheeks flushed, and she smiled shyly.

"Every word," I said, my voice low and firm. "You deserve the world, and I'm gonna give it to you."

By the time we hit 'Anthony's Steak House' the following Saturday, we were hitting our stride. She wore a sleek black dress that hugged her curves, and I couldn't keep my eyes off her. Every man in the restaurant stole glances, and I made sure they saw the way I held her close, letting them know she was mine.

"Don't you look good enough to eat," I murmured as we slid into the booth.

"You better behave, Legend." She rolled her eyes, but I caught the faint smile she tried to hide.

"What if I don't wanna?" I teased, leaning closer so my lips almost brushed her ear.

"You're impossible." She laughed, pushing me playfully.

"Only for you," I replied, grinning as I leaned back.

On our next date we ended the night at a new spot called 'Shanna's Bar & Grill', the dim lights and old-school R&B setting the perfect vibe. We danced close, her body fitting against mine like she was made for me.

"Ain't nobody else in this room but us, Dee," I whispered in her ear, as we swayed to the music.

A RATCHET CITY GOON'S THANKSGIVING CELEBRATION

"You always know what to say, don't you?" Her smile was soft, her hands resting on my chest.

"Not always," I admitted, my tone serious now. *"But I know what I feel. And right now, I feel like the luckiest nigga in the world."*

"I feel the same way." Her cheeks flushed, and she pressed her forehead to mine.

As the weeks passed, I found myself balancing my new job responsibilities with my growing relationship. My world was changing, and for the first time, it felt like I was building something tangible. Something real that I could believe in. And I'd do whatever it took to protect it.

THE SUN HAD DIPPED below the horizon, leaving a soft glow in the sky that painted the Jackson Heights Projects in hues of lavender and orange. Deandra's front porch was quiet, except for the faint chirping of crickets and the occasional shuffle of a neighbor walking by. The cinnamon scented candles she had burning inside wafted through the screen door, mixing with the earthy smell of the evening air. I sat back on the concrete steps, my long legs stretched out, while Deandra sat close beside me, her knee brushing mine.

Her presence was calming, but tonight, my mind was a storm. I stared out into the dimly lit street, hands clasped in front of me as my thoughts swirled.

"This new position..." I started, my voice low and steady, carrying a weight I didn't often let slip through. *"It means I can finally start providin' for my mom. She's worked two jobs her whole damn life, Dee. CNA at Spring Lake Guest Care and Heritage Manor South. She's been breakin' her back for as long as I can remember, just to keep me fed and clothed."* My jaw tightened as I spoke, the ache in my chest spilling into my words. *"I owe her everything."*

Deandra turned to me, her warm brown eyes softening with understanding. She reached for my hand, her small fingers intertwining with mine.

"You love her, she's your mom. So, that's understandable," she murmured, her voice gentle.

"Hell yeah, I do," I said, my voice thick with emotion. *"I've watched her struggle every day, Dee. Every single damn day. There were nights I'd wake up and*

hear her cryin', thinkin' I couldn't hear her. But I did. And it killed me, knowin' there wasn't shit I could do back then to help."

"This position with Stone's crew... it's gonna change things. I ain't just runnin' around anymore. This is a real setup, structure, money, a way outta this bullshit cycle. I can finally give her the life she deserves. Hell, I can give you the life you deserve." Deandra squeezed my hand, her touch grounding me.

"Legend, you're already giving me more than I've ever had. But I'm scared for you. This life... it's dangerous. What if something happens to you?" She leaned into me slightly, her voice low.

Her words hit me harder than I wanted to admit. I glanced at her, seeing the worry etched into her features, and I hated that my choices had put that fear in her. I looked away, my gaze fixing on the cracked sidewalk.

"You ain't wrong," I said finally, my voice quiet but firm. "This life? It is dangerous. But that danger? That's on me. It's part of what I signed up for. What I won't do, Dee, is let it touch you or my mom. That's what this whole thing is about. Y'all deserve more, and I'm gonna give it to you, no matter what it takes."

I leaned back against the porch railing, my shoulders loosening just a bit as I shifted gears.

"There's some things you gotta know, though, Dee. I can't ever talk to you about what I do. Pillow talk is off limits, Stone made that real clear, and I respect it. It's not just about protectin' the business; it's about protectin' you. The less you know, the safer you are." My voice softened, but it didn't lose its edge.

"I get it," she said quietly. "I just... I hate the idea of you carryin' all this by yourself." Her lips pressed into a thin line, and I could tell she wasn't thrilled, but she nodded.

"Dee, I ain't carryin' it by myself. Every time I look at you, every time I think about what we're buildin', that's what keeps me goin'. You're my reason, Dee. And as long as I got you, I can handle whatever comes my way." I turned to her, my gaze locking onto hers.

"I just don't want to lose you," Her eyes glistened, and she leaned into me, resting her head on my shoulder as she whispered, her voice breaking slightly.

"You won't," I said firmly. "I'm not goin' nowhere. We got somethin' solid here, Dee. I feel it. Don't you?"

"I do. I just... it's hard not to worry." She nodded, her hair brushing against my chin.

A RATCHET CITY GOON'S THANKSGIVING CELEBRATION

"I get that. And I ain't gonna sit here and act like I'm invincible. But I'm smart, Dee. I move careful. And everything I do, I do for you and my mom. Y'all are my priority." I kissed her forehead, letting my lips linger there for a moment.

"You really think we can build somethin' better?" Her voice was barely audible when she spoke again.

"I don't just think it, I know it. This ain't just me dreamin', Dee. This is real. We're gonna make it outta this. Together." I pulled her closer, my arm wrapping around her waist.

Listening to the crickets chirping in the distance and smelling the cinnamon scented air wrapped around us, I felt a rare sense of peace. Holding Deandra in my arms, I knew this was what I was fightin' for. Not just the money, not just the hustle, this. Her. Us. Together.

And no matter how dangerous the road ahead got, I knew I'd walk through fire to keep this safe.

CHAPTER SIX FINDING HERSELF AGAIN

I sat in my room, with my back against the wall and my knees pulled up to my chest. The familiar hum of the ceiling fan above me couldn't drown out the storm of emotions raging inside me. The past few weeks had been hectic. Legend started his new job, and his hours were wild. His phone stayed blowin' up all night, and he'd be jumpin' out of bed to handle all kinds of drama.

Still, no matter how crazy his schedule got, he always made time for me. At least twice a week, without fail, we'd step out to dinners, rides through the city, the two of us just vibin' together. And that was somethin' Corey never gave me. Five years with him, and not one real date. Hell, he'd fake like he was takin' me out, and then leave me hanging like it was nothin'. I still can't believe I allowed him to control my life like that.

"How did I let it go on for so long and get as bad as it did?" I muttered, the familiar pang of regret stabbing at my chest.

I rubbed my forehead, the weight of guilt heavy. I should've listened to my girls. I should've trusted them instead of turnin' my back on the people who actually had my back.

Raylexia, Winkie, Shamena, Johnya, and Deana, we were like sisters back then. Ride-or-die, no questions asked. And I threw all that away for some triflin' ass nigga who treated me like shit. My jaw clenched as the anger bubbled up inside me, not just at Corey, but at myself.

"How could I be so blind? So damn stupid?" I wanted to put all the blame on him, but deep down, I knew better. I stayed. I chose to believe his lies. I was the one who let him isolate me from the only real friends I had.

"What if they don't want to deal with me no more?" I thought my throat tight as fear crept in.

A RATCHET CITY GOON'S THANKSGIVING CELEBRATION

"What if it's too late to fix this?" I thought of them movin' on, livin' their best lives while I was stuck, playin' a fool for Corey and it was almost too much to take.

"Nah, I gotta try. I owe them that much, shit I owe it to myself," I clenched my fists, my nails diggin' into my palms.

Swallowin' my fears, I reached for my phone. My hands shook as I scrolled through my contacts. Finally, I landed on Winkie's name. My thumb hovered for a second before I pressed the call button.

The line rang once... twice... three times. My stomach knotted. Then her voice came through.

"Dee?" she said, surprise all over her tone. *"Damn, it's been a minute."*

My heart twisted up, guilt rushin' in.

"Hey, Wink," I whispered, my voice thick with emotion and barely holdin' steady. *"Yeah, it has. Look, I don't even know how to start this... but I'm sorry. For everything. For not listening. For choosin' Corey over y'all. I was so stupid, and... and I hate myself for lettin' him fuck up the friendship we had."*

The line went quiet, Winkie didn't speak and I held my breath, my heart poundin'.

"Was she about to hang up? Snap on me? I wouldn't even blame her if she did."

"Dee, we missed you. But we're not mad anymore," Winkie said softly, her voice carrying a mix of warmth and calm. *"We were hurt, yeah, but we've all moved on."*

"You moved on?" I echoed, my voice cracking, a fragile thread about to snap. Her words hit me hard, and before I knew it, tears were slipping down my cheeks, tears I wasn't even sure were from relief or sorrow.

"Yeah, we've all moved out of the old complex, and we're in new relationships, building new lives. But that don't mean we forgot about you," Winkie continued, her tone softening.

"Are... are you saying you're willing to let me back in?" My voice trembled as I clung to the hope flickering inside me. It felt fragile, but it was there, giving me just enough strength to hold on.

"Of course," Winkie said with a light chuckle. *"We've been waiting on you to call, girl. Raylexia told us you'd reach out once you got your mind right. I guess she was right about that."*

Her words sank in, but I still couldn't believe it. After everything, they were waiting for me. I bit my lip to keep from breaking down completely.

"I... thank you. I don't even know what to say, Wink. I fucked up so bad. I should've been there, I should've never..."

"Hold up," she cut in gently, but her tone carried a no nonsense vibe. "We all make mistakes, Dee. You ain't gotta beat yourself up about it forever. What matters is you're here now."

"I don't even know how y'all could forgive me after everything I did. I chose Corey over y'all, and y'all were my friends. The only real family I have. I was so stupid, Wink. I let that nigga run my life, isolate me, play me, and I pushed away the only people who really cared about me. It's like I let him win." The dam I was trying so hard to hold back cracked wide open.

"You didn't let him win," Winkie said, her voice firmer now. "You walked away, didn't you? That's a win, Dee. You might've taken a little longer to see the light, but you ain't stuck there no more. That's all that matters."

"I'm just scared, Wink. What if I fucked it up too bad? What if it's too late?" I wiped at my face, trying to keep my voice steady.

"It ain't too late. Trust me." She paused for a moment, and I could picture her on the other end, biting her lip like she did when she was trying to find the right words. "Look, Dee, we all got stuff we regret. You think I don't sit up some nights wonderin' if I did the right thing, leavin' the old neighborhood? Or if I should've tried harder to reach out to you when I saw you slippin' away? But life don't come with a rewind button. All we can do is move forward."

Her words penetrated deep, pulling at a part of me I'd been trying to ignore. She wasn't just being supportive, she was baring her own struggles, letting me see that she got it, that she understood in a way only my real friends could.

"What about you?" I asked, my voice soft, a little hesitant. "You said you moved on. What's new?"

"Girl, a lot. I'm workin' at this car lot now, don't laugh. All the salesmen actually love me, believe it or not. And I'm with someone too. He's low-key important in certain circles, and he's really good to me. We got together and moved fast, but I'm takin' it one step at a time getting to know the me I am with him, you know?" Winkie chuckled, and I could almost hear the smile in her voice.

A RATCHET CITY GOON'S THANKSGIVING CELEBRATION

"*That's good, Wink. You deserve that. You deserve everything.*" I smiled through my tears.

"*So do you, Dee,*" she said, her tone soft. "*You just gotta stop punishing yourself and start livin' again.*"

"Yeah," I whispered, nodding even though she couldn't see me. "*I've been trying. Legend's been helping me a lot. He's... different. I mean, he's got his own drama, but he makes time for me. He listens. Corey never did that. Not once.*"

"*Sounds like he's a keeper,*" Winkie said with a teasing lilt that made me laugh for the first time in what felt like forever. "*But don't let him carry all your baggage, Dee. You gotta heal for yourself.*"

"*I know,*" I said, swallowing hard. "*And part of that is fixin' things with y'all. If you'll let me.*"

"*Like I said, 'we've been waitin', girl,'*" she said, her voice warm again. "*How about this? We all hang out at a friend's spot, 'Shanna's Sports Bar & Grill'. It's chill, good food, good vibes. You can meet up with everybody, and we'll catch up.*"

"*I'd love that. More than anything,*" I said, a smile breaking through the tears that kept falling. For the first time in years, I felt like I was on the edge of recovering. Coming back from all the pain and suffering I allowed Corey to put me through.

"*Then it's a date,*" Winkie said, and I could hear the excitement in her voice. "*And Dee?*"

"Yeah?"

"*You don't gotta be perfect, alright? Just be you. That's all we ever wanted.*"

Her words settled in my chest like a warm blanket, and for the first time in a long time, I felt like I could breathe.

THE NEXT EVENING, I stepped into 'Shanna's Sports Bar & Grill', with my nerves buzzing with anxiety. The place was alive with activity and packed wall-to-wall with laughter and the scent of sizzling burgers and wings mixed with fried pickles and beer. My heart raced as my eyes scanned the room. Then I spotted them, my girls, crowded in the six large corner booths, their laughter and energy lighting up the space.

But instead of rushing over, I froze.

"What if they're different now? What if I don't fit in anymore?" The questions clawed at my mind, and for a split second, I thought about turning around and walking out.

Then Winkie's eyes locked on me, and she waved with a bright, knowing smile. My heart squeezed, and before I knew it, my own grin stretched wide across my face. Her acknowledging me had the desired effect of lightening my burden.

"Dee! Over here!" Winkie's voice rang out, soft yet commanding in its own way, full of warmth. She didn't even stand up, but somehow, her energy reached me like she was pulling me to herself.

I approached slowly, my steps unsure, but as soon as I saw their familiar faces, all my worries started to melt away.

"Hey, y'all," I said, my voice cracking as I fought back tears. *"I missed y'all so much."*

"Girl, we missed you too! Look at you, all grown and beautiful!" Johnya didn't hesitate. She was on her feet in seconds, wrapping me up in one of her tight, dramatic hugs that always made you feel like the most important person in the world.

Deana was next, her hand slipping into mine as her calm, steady presence immediately soothed me. My eyes dropped to her swollen belly, and I smiled wide.

"Damn, Dee, we got so much to catch you up on!" Deana's voice was gentle but brimming with excitement. *"Wait 'til you hear about our new lives."*

Raylexia smirked, raising a glass of Coke like it was champagne. *"Nah, wait 'til you hear about our new men,"* she teased with a wink, her no-nonsense tone laced with playfulness.

"You? A man? New men?" My eyebrows shot up, a laugh bubbling out before I could stop it. Raylexia was always too picky for her own good. She didn't like nobody, male or female. So, we used to joke she'd end up alone because she was A-Sexual. *"Now that's a new twist. Guess we all misjudged you."*

"Told y'all I had standards. I wasn't settlin'. But yeah, we all upgraded. Good men, Dee. Real ones. And guess what? Legend's workin' with our guys now. He's fitting right in." Raylexia leaned back with a confident grin, shrugging like what she'd just said was no big deal.

A RATCHET CITY GOON'S THANKSGIVING CELEBRATION

"Wait, what? My Legend? You're saying he's with your guys?" My jaw dropped, shock laced with pride.

"Yep." Raylexia gave me a knowing look. *"And he's solid, Dee. Handles his business like a pro. You know they don't tell us anything about their jobs, they keep us out of the messy stuff, but when we asked, 'cause we were worried about you, they made it clear he's doin' his job and doin' it well."*

Winkie nodded from her seat, her quiet demeanor steady as always. *"Ray even gave him her seal of approval,"* she added softly, her shy smile warming the edges of her words.

"Ray..." My voice trembled, emotions building up in my chest. *"You always had that sixth sense about people. I just wish I'd listened to you back then when we were twelve and you warned me about Corey. You were right, and I ignored you."*

"Dee, you were young. We all made mistakes. What matters is you learned. Corey? He was just a traffic stop on your way to where you were meant to be. Same way Zylar was a bump in the road for me." Raylexia's smirk softened into something more thoughtful.

"Zylar? Who's that? And wait, what happened with him?" I blinked, taken aback.

Raylexia leaned in, her no-nonsense tone dropping as she filled me in briefly. *"It's a long story. Too much for one night. But yeah, that chapter's closed. And you know what? It led me to Daylon. We're married now, Dee. Got kids too."* Her smile turned devilish, and the warmth of her words wrapped around me with the comfort of a hug.

"Daylon? You mean Day Day?" I whispered, memories flooding back. *"He's loved you since we were kids..."*

"And he still does. Crazy, right?" Raylexia laughed lightly, her outgoing energy shining through.

Before I could respond, my phone buzzed, and Shamena's face popped up on the screen. I answered, and her bright, lively voice filled the space as she proudly introduced me to her newborn son over video call. The little guy was precious, and my heart swelled as I congratulated her.

Meanwhile, Winkie stayed seated, her quiet, supportive energy grounding the chaos around us. When I finally asked why she hadn't gotten up, she blushed shyly.

"I just had my daughter last month. Ain't supposed to be out, but I wasn't about to miss this for nothin'. You're family, Dee."

That admission hit me hard, and I quickly insisted her husband take her home to rest. "Winkie, you didn't have to do this," I said, my voice thick with emotion.

"Yeah, I did," she replied softly. "You needed this. And we need you too."

By the end of the night, my phone was packed with new contacts, my heart fuller than it had been in years. As we laughed, ate, and caught up on life, the guilt and bitterness I'd carried for so long began to fade, replaced by something I hadn't felt in years, hope.

"This is what I've been missing," I whispered to myself, and for the first time in forever, I felt alive.

OVER THE NEXT WEEK, I found myself falling back into the rhythm of my girls' lives. It felt natural, like no time had passed at all, but so much had changed. We weren't the same girls from the old neighborhood, we'd grown and evolved. I soaked up every detail about their new lives, watching how their men moved around them with love and respect. They weren't just boyfriends or husbands; they were protectors, providers and partners. And I was there when Legend officially met my crew.

We'd gathered at Raylexia's enormous house for one of her famous fish fries. The laughter and energy filled the air as my nerves churned. Legend was his usual calm, steady self, but I couldn't help but feel like this was a test. Raylexia, as always, was the unspoken leader, and her approval carried weight.

As the night went on, I caught her watching Legend. Her sharp eyes, full of that no-nonsense energy, tracked his every move, the way he spoke, how he carried himself, how he interacted with the group. I tried to play it cool, but my heart was racing. Then, as Legend told a story about a crazy event he'd witnessed go down in the projects, Raylexia leaned back in her chair, a small smile tugging at her lips. She nodded, just once, and met my eyes.

"You did good, Dee," she said later, pulling me aside. Her voice was low, firm, but laced with warmth. "He's solid. I see it. He's got your back, and that's all I ever wanted for you. Just don't mess it up by second guessing yourself. You deserve this."

A RATCHET CITY GOON'S THANKSGIVING CELEBRATION

"Thank you, Ray. That means everything coming from you." Her words touched me deeply, and I felt a lump rise in my throat.

"Just keep him in check, though. Ain't nobody perfect." She shrugged like it was no big deal, but her smirk gave her away.

LATER THAT WEEK, LEGEND and I sat on my apartment porch, the air thick with the sound of crickets and the distant hum of the city. He reached for my hand, his touch warm and reassuring.

"You've been quiet tonight," he said, his voice low and gentle. *"What's on your mind?"*

"I've been thinking about how much has changed. Where I was just a few months ago compared to now. Meeting you, getting my girls back... it's overwhelming, but in the best way." I sighed, leaning my head against his shoulder.

"Dee, you ain't gotta carry all that weight by yourself anymore. I told you, I'm here. For the long haul. Whatever you need, I got you." Legend shifted, turning to look at me, his dark eyes steady and full of warmth.

His words wrapped around me like a blanket, and for the first time in years, I felt safe.

"I'm scared," I admitted softly. *"Scared I'll mess this up. Scared that I'll lose you too."*

"You ain't gonna lose me," he said firmly, pulling me closer. *"You think I came all this way just to let you go? Nah, Dee. I see you, the real you, and I ain't goin' nowhere. You just gotta let yourself believe it."*

"I'm so grateful for you, Legend. I don't know what I did to deserve you, but I'm glad you're here." His words settled deep, easing some of the doubts I didn't even realize I'd been carrying. I squeezed his hand, my heart full to bursting.

"You deserve everything, Dee. Don't ever question that." He smirked, his confidence shining through.

THE WEEK WASN'T JUST about me and Legend, though. The one-on-one time I spent with each of my girls and their men was just as healing.

First Legend and I spent time with Winkie and Karel or K-O. Winkie had been resting at home since she'd just had her baby, but K-O insisted we stop by. Their place was cozy, a nice four bedroom five bath in a secured gated community. They had baby toys and blankets scattered around, the little reminders of their new life. K-O, usually the quiet one, made sure Winkie had everything she needed. Him and Legend hovered in the background, watching us with a protective gaze while Winkie and I talked.

"You good, Dee?" Winkie asked softly, her shyness fading in the comfort of her own space.

"I'm getting there," I said honestly. "I missed this. Missed y'all."

"You're family," she said simply. "Family always finds its way back."

NEXT WE VISITED WITH Johnya and Zaylar or Stone as Legend calls him. Johnya had always been the bold, sneaky one, and Stone was her perfect match. They moved like a power couple, playful and intense all at once. We met up at Shanna's Sports Bar & Grill, and Johnya wasted no time getting into my business while Legend and Stone talked over by the pool table.

"So, what's the deal with you and Legend?" she asked, smirking. "You serious, or is he just a placeholder?"

"Johnya!" I laughed, but her question caught me off guard. "No, it's real. I've never felt like this before."

"Well, good," she said, leaning back. "But don't let him slack. A man's only as good as the woman holdin' him down, and you? You're a queen, Dee. Don't you forget it."

DEANA AND DAYTON OR Tone was our next visit. Deana's calm presence was a balm to my nerves when we met at her place. They stayed in the 'Belvin's Tower' on the penthouse floor shared with his other four brothers. I knew the Belvins' Brothers from the sports tournaments they hosted at the SPAR. So, Tone was familiar to me, and he and Legend walked off to his mancave.

Deana's belly was huge, and Dayton was practically her shadow, making sure she didn't lift a finger.

A RATCHET CITY GOON'S THANKSGIVING CELEBRATION

"I'm proud of you," Deana said, her hand resting on mine. *"You've come a long way, Dee. And Legend? He seems like the real deal."*

"He is," I said, my voice steady. *"I just hope I don't mess it up."*

"You won't," she said firmly. *"Because you know better now. And that's half the battle."*

THE NEXT VISIT WAS to Shamena and Cree or C-Lo's place. Shamena's new baby was the center of attention when we visited her. C-Lo was quiet, but his actions spoke volumes, always a step ahead of what she needed.

"You're in good hands now, Dee," Shamena said as she held her son. *"I see the way Legend looks at you. You're safe with him."*

RAYLEXIA AND DAYLON or Day Day was our last stop. Raylexia and Day Day had an energy that radiated love and stability. Watching them together was like watching a partnership that had weathered every storm.

"Take your time," Raylexia advised. *"You don't have to rush into nothin'. But if Legend's the one, don't let your fears hold you back."*

By the end of the week, I felt a sense of peace I hadn't known in years. Legend had seamlessly blended into my world, and with my friends' support, I finally felt like I could breathe again.

"This is it," I thought one night as Legend wrapped an arm around me. *"This is what it feels like to finally move forward."*

CHAPTER SEVEN
OPENING UP

The evening air was thick with the smell of fried food from the apartment down the way and the steady hum of the Allen Avenue traffic. Legend and I sat side by side on the porch of my apartment. From a distance I could hear the laughter of kids playing and the muffled voices of neighbors sounding through the air. My palms were sweaty, my hands trembling slightly as I tugged at the hem of my shirt. My heart pounded, and I could feel the heat rising in my face.

"He deserves to know," I thought, the words heavy in my mind. *"Even if it makes me look weak."*

Legend turned toward me, his dark brown eyes full of warmth and concern. He was like that, a quiet, steady presence that always seemed to notice when something wasn't right with me.

"You good?" he asked softly, his deep voice cutting through the noise in my head.

I swallowed hard, forcing myself to take a deep breath. The truth had been choking me for too long. It was time to get it all out in the open.

"No," I admitted, my voice shaky. *"I'm not."*

Legend reached over, his large hand covering mine, his touch grounding me in a way I didn't think was possible. But even with him sitting so close, the turmoil inside me refused to settle. I closed my eyes for a moment, feeling the weight of everything pressing down on my chest.

"I need to tell you some things," I began, my voice cracking. *"But not out here. Can we go inside?"*

Without hesitation, Legend stood and opened the apartment door, giving me space to walk in first. I locked the door behind us, more out of habit than

A RATCHET CITY GOON'S THANKSGIVING CELEBRATION

anything, and led him to my bedroom. The small, familiar space felt like a sanctuary and a prison all at once.

We both sat on the edge of my bed, and I stared down at my clenched fists in my lap, trying to find the right words. My breathing hitched as the memories clawed their way to the surface.

"This... this is about Corey," I finally said, my voice barely above a whisper. "About what he put me through, or should I say what I let him put me through."

"I'm listening." Legend didn't flinch, didn't press me to continue. He just nodded slightly, his gaze steady and full of patience.

"I spent five years trying to be enough for a nigga who didn't even deserve my time," I hissed, my anger building as I spoke. "Five years of lies. Five years of being made to feel like I wasn't good enough. Every time he cheated, every time he called me stupid, I stayed. I kept tryin' to fix something that wasn't never meant to be fixed." I drew in a shaky breath, my voice trembling as the words spilled out.

My throat tightened, and I forced myself to meet Legend's gaze. His expression didn't change, he was still calm, focused, absorbing every word like he understood this wasn't just me venting. This was me bleeding.

"I'm angry, Legend," I continued, my voice rising. "Angry at him for treating me like trash. But I'm even angrier at myself for letting it happen. For believing him when he said he'd change. For thinking if I just loved him harder, did more, was more, it would fix him." My hands shook and my fists clenched so tight my knuckles ached. "I wasted my love, my time, my happiness on someone who didn't deserve it. And now..."

"Now I'm scared. Scared you'll think I'm weak for staying as long as I did. Scared you'll look at me different when you see just how much of a mess I was." My voice broke, and I felt the sting of tears welling in my eyes.

I looked down, ashamed of my own words. My chest ached, the weight of my confession almost unbearable. But Legend didn't let go of my hand. His grip tightened just enough to remind me he was still there. Still with me.

"Dee, look at me." After a moment of silence, he shifted closer, his voice low and steady.

I hesitated, but when I finally lifted my gaze to meet his, his expression was so full of care it almost undid me completely.

"You ain't weak," he said, his voice firm but gentle. "You hear me? You ain't weak, and you damn sure ain't stupid. You're human. You loved somebody who didn't know what to do with that kind of love. That ain't on you."

"But I let him..." I bit my lip, trying to hold back the tears threatening to spill.

"Nah," Legend cut me off, his tone softening. "Don't do that. Don't blame yourself for his bullshit. You were young, Dee. You did what you thought was right at the time. And yeah, maybe you stayed longer than you should've, but you walked away. You chose yourself in the end. That's strength, baby. That's you winning."

I let his words sink in, my chest aching with a mixture of relief and lingering guilt.

"I'm just... I'm scared," I admitted, my voice breaking. "I don't ever wanna go back to feeling like that. Like I'm not enough. Like I'm worthless."

"Listen to me, Dee," he said, his voice low and full of conviction. "You're enough. You're more than enough. And I'll spend every damn day makin' sure you know that. I ain't Corey. I ain't gonna break you down or make you feel small. You're my queen, and I got you. Always." Legend leaned forward, resting his forehead against mine, his hands coming up to cradle my face.

"Thank you," I whispered. "For seeing me. For being here." The tears came then, silent and hot, spilling down my cheeks as I leaned into him.

"Ain't no thanks needed. I'm here, Dee. For the long haul. You don't have to fight this battle alone no more." Legend pulled me into his arms, his embrace strong and protective.

"You really don't think of me as weak?" I asked in a small voice.

"Dee," Legend's deep voice broke through my walls, steady and full of care. He reached up and cupped my face, his hands warm and grounding, like he was anchoring me in place. "Just like I said before, 'You are not weak. You're not stupid. You survived. You did what you had to do to get through it, and you came out stronger for it. Don't blame yourself for the choices you made when you were just tryin' to hold on."

His words broke something in me. A sob bubbled in my throat, and tears spilled down my cheeks faster than I could wipe them away. I tried to look away, to hide the mess I felt I was, but Legend wouldn't let me. His hands stayed on my face, his eyes locked on mine with so much understanding that it almost hurt.

A RATCHET CITY GOON'S THANKSGIVING CELEBRATION

"How is he so patient with me?" I wondered through the tears. *"How can he still see something good in me after everything I just told him?"*

"But what if I mess this up?" I choked out, my voice raw. *"What if all this baggage from Corey ruins what we have? I don't want to push you away because I can't let go of the past. I can't lose you, Legend."* My hands trembled as I balled my fists in my lap, the fear in my chest nearly suffocating me.

"Dee, you ain't gonna lose me. You think I don't know you're carryin' some heavy shit? You think I don't see what you been through? Baby, I see all of it. I see you. And none of it makes me wanna walk away. I'm here, for all of it. The good, the bad, the ugly, you don't gotta hide nothin' from me." Legend didn't waver. His jaw tightened, and he leaned closer, his voice low but firm.

His words made my tears fall harder.

"You mean that?" I whispered, my voice shaky.

"Every word," he said, his thumb brushing a tear from my cheek. *"You don't gotta be perfect for me, Dee. I ain't lookin' for that. What I want is you. The real you. And if the past comes up and you start feelin' that fear again, tell me. We'll work through it together, like we're doin' right now."*

"Thank you," I whispered, my voice breaking. *"I don't deserve you."* I stared at him, overwhelmed by the sincerity in his eyes. No one had ever spoken to me like that, like I was worth the effort, like I was enough just as I was.

"Stop sayin' that, Dee. You deserve everything I'm givin' and then some. You deserve a man who's gonna fight for you, who's gonna love you through all the pain and remind you that you're more than enough. And I'm that man. I'm not goin' nowhere. I refuse to even give another nigga a chance to try." Legend shook his head, his hands still cradling my face.

A soft, broken laugh escaped me through my tears, and I leaned into him, resting my forehead against his chest. His arms wrapped around me, holding me tight, and for the first time in years, I felt safe. Truly safe.

"I'm so grateful for you," I murmured, my voice muffled against his chest. *"I didn't think I could feel this way again. Like maybe... maybe I can finally move on. Maybe I can heal."*

"You can, Dee," he said, his voice low and steady. *"And I'll be right here with you, every step of the way. You're not in this alone anymore."*

As the silence stretched between us, his warmth seeped into me, spreading to places I didn't know had gone cold. For the first time in years, I felt like I was exactly where I was supposed to be. My thoughts raced as I let myself feel the hope growing inside me.

"Maybe," I thought, *"just maybe, Legend's the cure to everything I've been fighting for so long."*

I leaned back slightly, looking up at him. His lips curved into a small smile, and before I could stop myself, I pressed my lips to his. The kiss was soft at first, slow and full of unspoken emotions, but it quickly deepened. Legend's hands moved to my waist, pulling me closer, and a heat bloomed inside me, spreading through my veins.

The tension shifted, a different kind of energy crackling between us. I felt the need rising, urgent and undeniable, and before I could overthink it, I let it take over. Legend didn't hesitate, his hands moving to remove my shirt and then his own, his movements deliberate but full of care.

By the time he laid me down at the foot of the bed, the rest of the world had faded away. He feasted on me, his kisses and touch igniting every part of me until I was trembling beneath him. Just when I thought I couldn't take it anymore, he slid inside me in one swift, perfect motion, filling every part of me.

Our movements were slow at first, deliberate, like we were savoring every second. But then the pace picked up, each thrust taking me closer to the edge. When I finally fell over, gasping his name, he wasn't far behind, his release matching mine in a moment of raw, unfiltered connection.

Afterward, we collapsed into each other, tangled in the sheets and each other's arms. His embrace was warm, his breathing steady, and as I drifted off to sleep, I realized I'd found something I hadn't even known I was looking for, peace.

CHAPTER EIGHT THE COLLEGE DREAM

I sat cross-legged in the middle of my old apartment's cramped living room, surrounded by half-packed boxes, tingling with excitement. My entire life was in transition, and for once, it felt like it was moving forward instead of falling apart. Legend had asked me to move in with him, and here I was, boxing up my past for a shot at a future that felt like a dream.

Every now and then, I stopped packing to take it all in, letting the warmth of anticipation settle in my chest.

Around me, my girls, Raylexia, Shamena, Johnya, Shayla (Winkie), and Deana, were sprawled out, filling the tiny space with laughter and energy. It hadn't even been a full month since we reconnected, but the bond between us was still as tight as it had been when we were kids.

"Dee, I still can't believe you're gonna be at the University of Shreveport with us this winter!" Raylexia said, her voice loud and excited as she leaned forward. "Like, girl, do you realize how big this is? I'm so damn proud of you."

"I can't believe it either," I admitted, letting out a shaky breath. "It's like... everything's finally falling into place. Missing the fall semester sucked, but now I'm more focused. Legend keeps hyping me up, and my mom's been super supportive too. It's like they're both making sure I don't second guess myself." I couldn't help the big smile spreading across my face.

"That's how it's supposed to be!" Winkie said, nudging me with her elbow and grinning wide. "Legend's a real one for that. Ain't none of that Corey bullsh... in your life no more. That nigga didn't deserve you anyway. But look at you now! New plans, new energy, and a whole new attitude."

The mention of Corey made me pause, my fingers grazing the cardboard of a box I was sealing.

"Y'all know," I started softly, looking at my hands, *"he used to tell me I wasn't smart enough to do something like this. Always tearing me down, making me feel like nothing I did would ever be good enough. For years, I believed him. I really thought he was right."*

A hush fell over the room. Then Shamena reached over, gripping my hand tight.

"But you don't believe that bullshit no more, right? Look at yourself, Dee. Legend ain't just been gassing you up, he's showing you the truth. You got this light in you, girl, and we all see it. That bitch nigga Corey tried to dim it, but you're shinin' brighter than ever now." The love and sincerity in her words made my throat tighten.

"It's not just Legend, though. It's y'all too," I said, my voice trembling with emotion. *"I forgot what it felt like to have people in my corner, rooting for me. Like, really rooting for me."*

"That's because we got you, Dee," Deana chimed in, her tone warm and reassuring. *"You're family, and family holds each other down. Plus, you're not doing this alone. We're all out at Shreveport, grinding and making it happen. You're about to be a part of that."*

"Exactly! I'm doing business management and accounting, Shamena's also taking business management, Deana's doing fashion design, Winkie's taking interior design, and Johnya's in the nursing program. So, you already got a squad waiting for you on campus." Raylexia nodded, her violet eyes lighting up.

"I'm so lucky to have y'all," I whispered. *"And I'm so ready for this. I wanna show everybody, especially myself, that I'm more than what Corey said I was. And I couldn't have done this without Legend or y'all."* I blinked back tears, shaking my head in disbelief.

"Speaking of Legend... moving in with him? Are you sure about that? 'Cause you know once you cross that line, it's real." Raylexia leaned forward, a knowing smirk on her face.

"I'm sure, Ray. Legend's different. He's got this way of making me feel safe, but not just that, he pushes me to be better. He sees things in me I didn't even see in myself." I met her gaze, her words carrying a weight I knew she didn't take lightly.

A RATCHET CITY GOON'S THANKSGIVING CELEBRATION

"Alright then. You got my stamp of approval. Just make sure he keeps treating you like the queen you are, or you know we'll pull up." Raylexia studied me for a long moment, then smiled.

The laughter that followed eased the tension in the room, and I felt a renewed sense of confidence. The conversation flowed easily after that, with everyone hyping me up about my move, my plans, and the fresh start waiting for me. For the first time in forever, I felt like I wasn't just surviving, I was thriving.

A knock on the door broke through our laughter, and I jumped up to answer it. When I opened it, there stood Legend, his tall frame leaning casually against the doorframe, a smirk playing on his lips.

"What's up, ladies?" he greeted, stepping inside and giving me a quick kiss on the forehead. *"Y'all taking care of my girl?"*

"Boy, please," Winkie shot back with a laugh. *"We're making sure she don't run off on you."*

"Good. 'Cause I'd be lost without her in my life." Legend chuckled, sliding his arm around my waist.

Legend pulled me closer, his voice dropping low so only I could hear.

"You good? Need me to do anything?" I felt my cheeks heat up as my friends erupted into playful teasing.

"You just being here is enough." I shook my head, smiling up at him.

After a little more joking and chatting, my friends started to gather their things to leave. As they headed out, each one of them hugged me tight, whispering words of encouragement and love. When the door closed behind the last of them, I turned to Legend, my heart full.

"You sure you're okay?" he asked, brushing a strand of hair from my face.

"I'm more than okay," I said, wrapping my arms around his neck. *"I've got you. I've got my friends. And for the first time in forever, I feel like I've got me too."*

And in that moment, as I rested my head on his shoulder in the arms of the man who had already become my safe place, I knew deep in my soul I was exactly where I needed to be.

A FEW DAYS LATER, I found myself standing in the front yard of a gorgeous home in the Southern Hills Subdivision, a place I never thought I'd see up close, much less be a part of. Legend had surprised his mother, Evelyn Boyd, with this brand new house, and I couldn't stop smiling, my chest full of happiness. The house was a breathtaking sprawling two story masterpiece with white stone accents, a huge front porch, and landscaping so perfect it looked like it belonged in a magazine. It wasn't just a house; it was a statement. A testament to how far Legend had come and the love he had for his mom.

Inside, the open floor plan stretched wide, with gleaming hardwood floors that shone like glass. The kitchen was straight out of a cooking show, complete with a massive island and state of the art appliances. The living room was cozy but elegant, with a towering stone fireplace that tied the space together. Legend had furnished every room with new, high end pieces, that were modern but comfortable. It felt like a dream brought to life.

Evelyn Boyd walked through the house, her hands covering her mouth, her steps slow as though she didn't believe this was real. Tears shimmered in her eyes, and her voice trembled when she finally spoke.

"Oh, my baby," she whispered, shaking her head in disbelief. *"I never thought I'd live to see the day we'd have something like this. It's more than I ever dreamed of Legend."*

"You deserve it, Ma. You always did. All the years you held it down, working two or three jobs just to keep a roof over my head and food on the table. You did that. Now it's my turn to take care of you." Legend stood tall, his chest puffed with pride as he watched her.

"I'm so proud of you, Legend. I'm so very proud. You've turned into the kind of man any mama would be blessed to have." Evelyn's tears spilled over, and she reached up to pull him into a hug.

I stood nearby, watching the two of them with my heart swelling with pride for Legend in my chest. Legend caught my eye and reached for my hand, pulling me closer to them.

"Dee," he said, his voice low and warm, *"this right here? This is part of what I've been grinding for. Myron helped me find this spot, made sure it's in a gated community so Ma'll be safe. It feels good, you know? Knowing she's finally got a place she can relax in."*

A RATCHET CITY GOON'S THANKSGIVING CELEBRATION

"It's beautiful, Legend. It's a reflection of how much you love her. She deserves this, and so do you. You've been working so hard and seeing this come to life is inspiring." I nodded, my throat tight with emotion.

"Speaking of deserving things," he said, "I heard from Shamena that you're officially moving forward with enrolling at Shreveport. I'm proud of you too, Dee. For real." He smiled at me, his gaze soft.

The pride in his voice made me blush.

"I still can't believe it's finally happening," I admitted, looking down for a moment before meeting his eyes again. "And having you and my mom push me to go for it? It means everything. It's so different from how it was with Corey. He never believed in me." I answered.

"I really don't like hearin' about that clown ass nigga. You know I'd stomp him out if I ever see him again, right? But for now, I'll let it slide, this time." Legend's jaw tightened, and his voice dropped to a growl.

Evelyn, standing behind him, reached up and smacked the back of his neck lightly.

"Boy, stop actin' a fool," she said, shaking her head. Then her focus shifted to me, her eyes full of warmth and wisdom. "Deandra, you're doing exactly what you're supposed to be doing. You've got a good head on your shoulders, and you're making moves that'll change your life for the better. Don't let anybody tell you otherwise."

"Thank you, Mrs. Boyd. That really means a lot." Her words hit me straight in the heart, and I could only nod as tears welled up in my eyes.

"You call me Ma, just like Legend does. We're family now, baby. And family supports each other." Evelyn stepped closer, patting my shoulder with a motherly touch.

"Okay... Ma. Thank you." The kindness in her tone undid me, and I couldn't stop the tears from falling. I laughed through the emotion, wiping my face.

"Ma, I gotta say this while we're all standing here. Everything I am today is 'cause of you. You sacrificed so much for me, stuff I didn't even realize at the time. You worked yourself to the bone, went without just so I could have what I needed. I ain't never gonna forget that. This house? This is just the beginning of me trying to pay you back." Legend wrapped his arm around my shoulders, pulling me close as he looked at his mother.

"*Legend, I didn't do it for payback. I did it because I love you, because I wanted you to have a chance at a better life. But seeing you become the man you are today? That's all the reward I'll ever need.*" Evelyn's lips trembled as more tears slipped down her face.

The three of us stood in the living room for a moment, the weight of our shared history filling the space. Then Evelyn wiped her eyes and clapped her hands.

"*Alright now! Enough crying. Let's get these boxes moved in so I can start making this house a home.*"

As we carried box after box inside, I felt a happiness I hadn't known in years. My past with Corey no longer loomed as heavily over me, and the anticipation of a better future fueled my every step. Watching Legend with his mother, feeling the love and pride, they shared for each other, reminded me of how much my life had changed since meeting him.

"*I'm finally where I'm supposed to be,*" I thought, my heart full. "*With the right people, making the right moves. And I'm ready to make the most of it.*" I glanced at Legend as he placed a box on the counter, his face glowing with satisfaction.

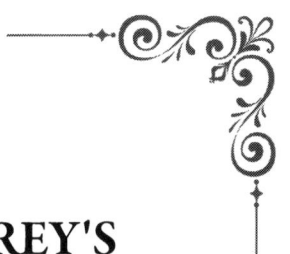

CHAPTER NINE COREY'S REALITY CHECK

I pulled up to the new spot, 'Shanna's Sports Bar & Grill', with Teresa clinging to my arm like some damn trophy. Truth be told, my mind wasn't on her or how good she looked in her tight black dress tonight. Nah, my focus was somewhere else entirely. Word on the street was that Dee, my Deandra, has been hanging out here on weekends with her little crew of aggravating ass friends. Call me a stalker if you want to, but I was determined to get my girl back. Teresa was just a pawn in my plan, even though she ain't got nothing on Dee. Never did.

The only reason I entertained these other females was because Dee never let me hit. Yeah, five years together, and she refused to go there with me. I thought flaunting other chicks would push her to finally give it up, but all it did was backfire. Now here I was, plotting my comeback. What really had me heated was knowing Dee went and gave it up to Legend in less than a week. Less than a damn week! That was a slap in the face if I ever felt one.

"Wow, Corey! This place is nice. Where'd you hear about it?" Teresa asked, her eyes darting around the room like she'd never been out before.

"One of my boys over here in Cedar Grove told me about it. Said they got good wings and burgers," I lied smoothly. It was my first time here too, but I wasn't about to admit that. I needed to keep control of the situation.

"Well, I'm glad we came..." Teresa started, but her words died in her throat. I turned to follow her gaze and felt my blood run cold.

There she was.

Deandra walked in, looking finer than I'd ever seen her, with Legend right behind her. She wore a fitted dress that hugged her curves, her natural hair bouncing as she moved. Legend's hand rested lightly on the small of her back, like he was staking his claim. I clenched my jaw as my eyes darted around the bar. It wasn't just her and Legend. Dee had her whole squad with her, Raylexia, Shamena, Johnya, Winkie, and Deana and all of them were posted up in a set of six booths in the corner. The energy around them was electric, like the whole bar revolved around their tables.

Scanning the room further, I spotted some heavy hitters posted up. Stone was near the pool table with C-Lo, Myron, Jamie, Lance, and Kam. The Belvins brothers were over by the dartboards, kicking it with K-O, Jayce, K-Boy, Killian, Khiershan, Blade, and Steel. That's when it clicked, the rumors were true. After King Michael cut Legend loose, Stone picked him up. Now, he was rubbing shoulders with some of the most respected names in Ratchet City.

"How the hell did this nigga go from getting cut to leveling up like this?" I fumed silently. *"And is Dee the reason he got on?"*

I didn't have long to dwell on it because Legend escorted Dee to the booth and kissed her before stepping away to dap up the guys at the pool table. Watching how easily he fit in with them made my stomach churn. The respect they showed him, the camaraderie, it all pissed me off. I should've been the one sitting at that booth with Dee, but I fumbled the bag.

"Corey, where do you want to sit?" Teresa asked, snapping me back to reality. I realized we were still standing awkwardly near the entrance, looking like idiots. I nodded toward the bar and led her over, choosing a spot where I could keep an eye on both Dee and Legend.

Teresa grabbed a menu, her excitement bubbling as she rattled off all the options. I didn't hear a word she said. My focus was locked on Legend. That nigga was moving through the room, stopping by every group, making connections. Each time he circled back to the booth, he'd lean down and kiss Dee like it was second nature. And the way she looked at him? It was like that nigga walked on fuckin' water. Her smile was blinding, her body language soft and open. She had never looked at me like that before. Not once in our five years together.

"She's happier without me," I admitted bitterly to myself, the thought cutting deep.

Then Teresa's voice broke through my haze.

"Really, Corey? Did you seriously bring me here just to spy on Deandra?" She hissed.

A RATCHET CITY GOON'S THANKSGIVING CELEBRATION

"You brought me here to watch her, didn't you? You're pathetic! You're still hung up on her after all this time, and you're using me to play your little games. Nigga, what's wrong with you?" I turned to face her, but before I could speak, she went off, her voice loud enough to draw attention.

"Teresa, keep your damn voice down," I growled, feeling the weight of the stares from everyone in the bar.

"Nah, fuck that!" she snapped, standing up from her stool. *"You always talking about how Deandra begged you to stay with her. But you know what? I'm starting to see it was you all along. You couldn't let her go. She's moved on, Corey! Look at her! She's happy. She's with a real man now. And here you are, dragging me into this shit, trying to make her jealous or whatever the hell this is. I'm done. Lose my number, nigga. You're trash."*

She snatched her purse off the bar and stormed out, leaving me sitting there looking like a fool. The room went quiet for a moment, and I felt every pair of eyes on me. Dee and her friends were looking too, but Legend? He wasn't even fazed. He stood across the room, watching me with a calm confidence that made my blood boil.

I stayed a minute longer, casting Dee one last lingering glance. She didn't look angry or smug, just indifferent. Like I didn't exist anymore. That hurt worse than everything Teresa said.

As I walked out, I couldn't shake the thoughts swirling in my head. I had Dee for five years, and I let her slip through my fingers. I controlled her every move, I manipulated her to think she was nothing special, I isolated her from her friends and family, and all for what? To prove a point? I should've treated her better. I should've listened to her, supported her dreams, and been the man she needed. But I wasn't. And now, Legend had everything I'd thrown away.

"I'll get her back," I muttered to myself as I stepped out the bar and into the cool night air. *"No matter what it takes. I'm going to get my bitch back."*

AFTER COREY AND TERESA stormed out of the bar, my friends surrounded me in a protective circle. Raylexia was the first to speak, her voice full of concern.

"Dee, are you okay?" she asked, her brows furrowed in worry.

Before I could answer, Legend was there. His presence was immediate and commanding. He moved with the kind of confidence that demanded attention, his tall frame cutting through the crowd effortlessly.

His dark eyes scanned me, and when he saw I was shaken, his expression softened, but only for me. To everyone else, he was a force to be reckoned with, his menacing aura a mix of danger and raw, magnetic appeal.

"We'll be back in a minute, y'all," Legend said over his shoulder, his deep voice steady as he scooped me out of the booth like I weighed nothing. He didn't wait for a response, and nobody dared to question him.

As we made our way outside, he grabbed both our coats from the rack with one hand, keeping me close with the other. The chill of the night air hit me, but before I could shiver, he was wrapping me up in my coat and guiding me toward his car, his sleek black Monte Carlo that gleamed under the streetlights looking like polished obsidian.

Legend opened the passenger door and sat down, pulling me onto his lap. His arms encircled me, shielding me from everything outside.

"Talk to me, Dee. You good?" he asked, his voice low and intimate, vibrating against my back as he rested his chin on my shoulder.

"I'm good, but I'll admit, I don't get it. Why not just be with those other hoes and move on? Why is he steady coming around me? It makes no sense." I took a shaky breath, my thoughts jumbled and chaotic.

"That's 'cause that nigga is lost right now. You had him cocky, Dee. He never thought you'd actually get tired of his bullshit. You gave up your friends for him, and he figured it was all good, like he had you locked down. But nah, you hit him with a reality check, and now he's sick. And he's gonna stay sick for a while." Legend chuckled, the sound dark and rich, with an edge that sent a shiver down my spine.

The way he said it, like Corey's misery was a foregone conclusion, made me laugh despite myself. Legend always had this way of making me feel like no one could touch me when I was with him.

"Unless I kill his punk ass and put him out his misery, that is." But then his voice dipped even lower, his tone sharper.

I stiffened slightly, tilting my head to look at him. His jaw was set, and there was a dangerous glint in his eyes that sent a warning to anyone thinking of crossing him. But then he noticed my concern and softened immediately.

A RATCHET CITY GOON'S THANKSGIVING CELEBRATION

"I'm serious though, Dee. Are you good? 'Cause I know this shit's gotta be draining for you," he added, his hand rubbing slow circles on my back.

"I'm good," I said, but my voice wavered. I hesitated before continuing. "It's just... I don't want you getting in trouble because of him. I know how you are, and I know you'd do anything to protect me. But I can't have you risking yourself because Corey can't take a hint."

"Dee, listen to me. There ain't no way I'm letting that nigga keep popping up and disrespecting you, us, or me. But I'm not about to do something stupid and leave you out here without me, either. I'm too invested in us, baby. You don't gotta worry about me." Legend tilted my chin up so I was looking directly at him.

His gaze was steady, intense, and filled with something that made my heart ache in the best way. His words wrapped around my heart like a safety net, but the thought of Corey still gnawed at me.

"I don't get why he even bothers. He had his chance, for five long years, Legend. Five years of me giving everything I had to someone who couldn't even see my worth. I don't want him back. I don't even want to be in the same room as him. And yet, here he is, trying to pull me back into his chaos." I sighed, leaning into Legend's chest. His scent, something warm, spicy, and uniquely him, filled my senses, grounding me. "I'm done with him. I don't even feel anything when I see him now. No love, no anger, no hurt. Just... nothing."

"That's 'cause you're over him, Dee. You're too busy moving forward to look back. And you ain't doing it alone, either. You got me, you got your girls, you got people who actually give a damn about you." Legend pressed his lips to my temple, the gesture soft despite the intensity radiating from him.

His words settled over me, a balm to my soul, soothing the last of my lingering doubts. He was right. I wasn't just surviving anymore, I was thriving. And that was because of him, because of the way he supported me without hesitation.

"Thank you, Legend. For everything. For making me feel like I'm enough." I looked up at him, a small smile tugging at my lips.

"Dee, you ain't just enough. You're everything. Now, let's talk about something better. Have you finished packing? When are we moving into our new spot?" His eyes softened, and he grinned, a dimple flashing on the right side of his jaw.

"You know I don't want to leave my mom alone for the holidays. So, after Thanksgiving." I laughed, the sound breaking through the silent parking lot.

He nodded, but his expression turned thoughtful, like he was already working on a plan.

WHAT DEE DIDN'T KNOW was that I had Myron scouting houses for her mom closer to our new spot. I wasn't just thinking about Deandra, I was thinking about our whole family too.

Dee and I stayed like that for a while, talking about everything and nothing until she shivered. I noticed instantly, pulling her to her feet and wrapping my arm around her.

"Let's get you back inside before you freeze," I said, my voice low and full of affection.

As we stepped back into the bar, the warmth and laughter of her friends greeted us. I could tell she felt lighter, freer even. I kissed her forehead before letting her rejoin her friends to say goodnight, my protective presence never too far away. Whatever storm was coming, I knew the two of us would face it together.

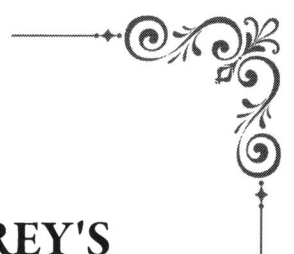

CHAPTER TEN COREY'S FINAL STUNT

I sat on the edge of my bed, my phone on speaker as me and Legend planned for our Thanksgiving holiday. The warm scent of cinnamon and vanilla candles filled the air, wrapping me in a sense of peace. Legend's voice came through the phone, smooth and full of excitement, the sound making me smile.

"I can't wait for Thanksgiving," he said, a grin evident in his tone. "Ma's already talking about making her famous cornbread dressing, and that coupled with your mom's pecan pie. Man, I've been dreaming about that," his enthusiasm catchy.

"I'm telling you, that pecan pie is going to win Ma over for sure. We're all gonna eat ourselves into a food coma." I laughed, catching his vibe, my heart light.

"I ain't even mad about it. Food coma, good vibes, and both our moms under the same roof? That's what family feels like, Dee." His words wrapped around my heart, warming me from the inside.

"Yeah, it really does," I said softly. "This is the first time I've been this excited for the holidays in... well, ever."

As we talked about dishes, games, and my idea to decorate our apartment with fall themed garlands, a sudden, loud knock at the door broke the moment. My body tensed, my heart pounding out of nowhere.

"Hold on, Legend, somebody's at the door," I said, picking my phone up as I headed to the door. I noticed it was cracked slightly, but before I could see who it was, the door flew open, slamming against the wall.

Corey stood there, his eyes wild, his chest heaving like he ran all the way here. Before I could react, his hand shot out, grabbing my arm with a grip that sent a jolt of panic through me.

"Corey, what the hell? Let me go!" I yelled, my voice sharp with fear. My phone clattered to the floor, Legend's voice shouting my name through the speaker.

Corey's grip tightened as he yanked me into the hallway, dragging me toward the stairs. My pulse thundered in my ears as I stumbled, struggling against his hold.

"Dee, listen to me!" he begged, his voice shaky and desperate. "*I just need to talk to you. Please! You gotta hear me out.*"

"*You're out of your damn mind!*" I shouted, panic swelling in my chest as I tried to pull free. "*You're hurting me! Let go!*"

The narrow hallway echoed with my protests, and neighbors began to poke their heads out of their doors. People murmured, some pulling out their phones to record, while others shouted at Corey to let me go.

"Man, let her go!" one man yelled. "*You trippin', bruh. She don't want yo' ass no more!*"

"Somebody call the police!" another woman screamed.

"Dee, you don't get it. I can't lose you! I know I messed up, but I love you. I can't let you go." Corey ignored them all, his grip like a vice on my arm. His eyes were locked on me, wide and frantic.

"You don't love me, Corey!" I spat, my voice shaking with fury. "*You never did. You just wanted to control me, to keep me under your thumb. I'm done! Find somebody else to manipulate 'cause I'm over you.*"

"No, Dee. You don't mean that. I need you! I'll change, I swear. Just give me another chance." Corey's face contorted with anguish, but his grip didn't loosen.

"*You've been saying that for years, and it's always been a lie! Even if you could change, I wouldn't want you. You're a liar, a cheater, and a coward, Corey. I'm finally free of you, and you're not taking that away from me!*" The fear in my chest turned into a simmering rage.

Tears burned in my eyes as I said the words, the finality of them washing over me. I was done. Truly done. But Corey wasn't ready to accept that. His grip turned rougher, and he sneered at me.

"*You think you're better off with that thug Legend?*" he hissed, his voice dripping with venom. "*You think he's gonna treat you right? He's just using you.*"

"*Legend is more of a man than you'll ever be!*" I shot back, my voice raw with rage. "*He loves me. He respects me. That's something you never did.*"

A RATCHET CITY GOON'S THANKSGIVING CELEBRATION

Just then, the crowd parted, and I saw Legend storming toward us. His tall frame moved like a predator stalking prey, his dark eyes blazing with an intensity that sent a chill through me. He radiated danger, his presence so commanding that the crowd instinctively stepped back.

"*Get your fucking hands off her,*" Legend growled, his voice deadly calm.

"*Or what? You gonna fight me again? You think you can just take what's mine?*" Corey sneered, still clutching my arm.

"*She ain't yours, nigga. She ain't been yours for a while now. Now let her go before you make me do something we're both gonna regret.*" Legend's eyes narrowed, his voice dropping lower.

Corey's grip faltered, and he shoved me away suddenly. As I stumbled back, he pulled a gun from his waistband, pointing it directly at Legend. Gasps rippled through the crowd, and my heart stopped.

"*I'll shoot you!*" Corey shouted, his hand trembling. "*Back the fuck off!*"

"*Put the gun down, Corey,*" Legend said, his voice steady. "*You ain't that guy. You know it, I know it, and everybody here knows it. You ain't built like that.*" Legend didn't flinch. His expression remained calm, though his eyes burned with fury.

"*You think you're better than me? You think you can take her away and everything's gonna be fine?*" Corey's hand shook, his grip on the gun unsteady.

"*I ain't here to take nothin' from you. But if you ever touch her again, I'll end you.*" Legend took a deliberate step forward.

The tension snapped as Legend lunged, tackling Corey to the ground. The gun flew out of Corey's hand, skidding across the pavement. The two of them grappled, Legend's fists flying as he pinned Corey down with sheer strength.

"*Stop! Somebody call the police!*" a voice from the crowd yelled.

"*You ever put your hands on her again, and I'll make sure you don't get back up.*" Legend's voice was a low growl, full of menace.

"*Dee, I'm sorry. Please. I love you.*" Corey sobbed, his face bloodied and broken.

"*You don't get to say that to me. You don't get to hurt me and then claim you love me. It's over, Corey. It's been over.*" I stepped forward, my voice shaking but firm.

"*Stay down,*" Legend growled, his voice low and menacing. He turned to the crowd, his glare silencing anyone still murmuring. "*Show's over. He's calm now.*"

One by one, the bystanders nodded and started to disperse, though not without lingering glances and whispered comments. Corey lay on the ground, groaning as the last few people stepped around him.

Legend still holding Corey down, turned to me, his dangerous aura softening as his gaze met mine. *"You good?"* he asked, his voice deep and gentle now.

"Yeah... *I'm good now,*" I nodded, though my hands trembled slightly as I looked down at him.

"Good," he said, still holding Corey in place.

The sound of sirens filled the air, and relief washed over me as the police arrived, arresting Corey for assault and attempted kidnapping. My knees buckled, and I collapsed into Legend's arms, sobbing as the adrenaline drained from my body.

Slipping an arm around my waist and pulling me closer. His presence, strong and steady, was everything I needed in that moment. As we walked away, I didn't look back. Corey was my past, and I was done letting him steal even one more second of my peace. Legend? He was my future, and I'd never been so sure of anything in my life.

"I got you, Dee," he whispered, holding me close. His hands stroked my back, his voice a soothing balm. *"You're safe now. I promise."*

As I clung to him, I felt the weight of the past finally lift. Corey was gone, and with Legend by my side, I was free. Free to heal, free to love, and free to move forward.

CHAPTER ELEVEN
THANKSGIVING CELEBRATION WITH FRIENDS

Shanna's Sports Bar & Grill was alive, buzzing with laughter, music, and the rich aroma of good food. The warm, golden glow from autumn garlands and strings of lights made the space feel cozy, almost magical. The place was packed with our closest friends and family, creating the kind of Thanksgiving I never thought I'd experience.

Legend stood beside me, his hand resting possessively on my waist. His presence was magnetic, his dangerous, confident aura drawing glances from across the room. In his tailored black hoodie and fitted jeans, he radiated raw sex appeal, a blend of menace and charm that made him irresistible. But when his gaze turned to me, his dark eyes softened, and the walls I kept up around everyone else crumbled.

I glanced at him, my heart swelling with emotion. This man wasn't just my love, he was my safe place, my calm in the chaos.

"You good?" he asked, his voice low, meant only for me.

"Better than good," I replied smiling, leaning into him.

Our moms, Andrea Jordan and Evelyn Boyd, stood a few feet away, chatting like lifelong friends. I couldn't help but grin as my mom gestured animatedly, recounting a story that had Evelyn laughing so hard she had to hold her side.

"Mom," I called, catching her attention. *"You tried the sweet potato pie yet?"*

"Not yet," mom said, her eyes lighting up. *"But you know I'm making room. I've never met a sweet potato pie I didn't like."*

"*You better hurry up,*" Evelyn chimed in, smirking at Legend. "*This one here's already on his third slice.*"

"*What can I say? It's fire.*" Legend grinned, shrugging unapologetically.

"*If you eat it all, we're gonna have a problem.*" I nudged him playfully.

"*The only problem is I can't get enough of you either.*" He pulled me closer, his lips brushing my ear.

I rolled my eyes, heat rising to my cheeks, but I couldn't stop smiling. Legend's ability to shift from tender to teasing, from intimidating to indulgent, was one of the many things that made him impossible to resist.

Across the room, the guys were posted up around the pool table and dartboards, their banter loud and unfiltered. Stone leaned against the table, a smirk playing on his lips as Day Day lined up his shot.

"*Day Day, you aiming for the pocket or the ceiling? Take the damn shot already,*" Stone teased, earning a round of laughter.

"*Nigga don't rush me. Precision takes time,*" Day Day shot back, squinting at the cue ball.

"*Better not miss after all that concentration,*" Myron added, clapping him on the back.

At the dartboards, Nico was locked in a tense match with Dayquan. Kam provided running commentary, his voice carrying over the music.

"*Yo, Nico, are you aiming, or just throwing and praying, bruh?*"

The girls were huddled in the cozy sitting area, their conversation just as lively.

"*Y'all remember sneaking into the YWCA pool after hours? We thought we were untouchable.*" Raylexia leaned forward, laughing as she recalled an old story.

"*We were slick,*" Shamena agreed, giggling. "*Until Ray's no-swimming ass got caught first. That man acted like we committed a federal crime.*"

"*He still brings it up every time he sees me. Calls me trouble like it's my middle name.*" Winkie grinned.

The laughter was infectious, and I felt a pang of gratitude for these women who had stuck by me through everything. They were more than friends, they were family.

A RATCHET CITY GOON'S THANKSGIVING CELEBRATION

"Whoever made that mac and cheese deserves an award. I had two helpings and still want more." The conversation shifted to food, and Deana sighed contentedly.

"That was my mama. Grandma's recipe. You're welcome." Winkie raised her hand proudly.

"Girl, she did that," Nisha said, nodding. *"That mac and cheese is the shit."*

As the night wore on, we all gathered near the bar for a toast. Legend pulled me close, his hand sliding down to rest on my hip. The energy in the room shifted as everyone quieted, the moment heavy with love and appreciation.

"I'll start," Raylexia said, holding up her glass. *"I'm thankful for all of you. For laughter, for memories, and for this amazing food. But mostly, I'm thankful for the way we've all stuck together through everything."*

"Facts," C-Lo agreed, raising his glass. *"Ain't nothing like family, blood or not."*

"Here's to the real ones," Legend said, his voice commanding attention. He looked down at me, his eyes softening. *"And to finding the kind of love that makes all the bullshit worth it."*

"To love, family, and new beginnings," I added, my voice trembling with emotion. My chest tightened, and I blinked back tears as everyone raised their glasses.

As the night went on, the girls decided to perform an impromptu R&B medley, complete with harmonized vocals and dramatic choreography. Raylexia and Johnya led the charge, their voices blending beautifully, while Shamena, Winkie and Deana provided backup vocals sitting down in the booth. The entire room clapped and cheered, the joy so thick you could feel it.

"You happy?" Legend leaned down, his lips brushing my ear.

"More than I ever thought I could be," I said, my voice thick with emotion. *"I feel so blessed."*

"You deserve all of it, Dee. And we ain't even scratched the surface yet," he murmured, pressing a kiss to my temple.

The night ended with heartfelt toasts from the elders, their words of wisdom grounding us in love and community. As the crowd began to disperse, Legend pulled me close again, his eyes locking onto mine with an intensity that made my pulse quicken.

"You know this is just the beginning, right?" he asked, his voice low and full of promise.

"I know." I nodded, a soft smile playing on my lips.

And as we stood there, surrounded by the laughter of our friends and family, I knew without a doubt that I was exactly where I was meant to be. The past was behind me, and the future, our future, was brighter than I could have ever imagined.

KING MICHAEL LEANED back in his leather chair, his voice heavy with tension as he was finally able to get Stone to pick up the phone.

"Yo, Stone, I need you to holla at Legend ASAP," he said, his tone cold but urgent. "Melody Jenkins, the lil chick he used to mess with, got beat down bad tonight, man. They left her for dead, the shit was straight up brutal. But here's the thing... she was pregnant and they managed to deliver his kid, dawg. Baby boy came too early, and now he's over at University Health fightin' for his life in the NICU. Premature, bruh, but the lil' man got Legend's blood in him, so he needs to know. I ain't even gotta say how deep this runs, but it all traces back to Jamaican Jay and his crew. Him and his boys out here reckless, no respect, and they crossin' lines that don't need crossin'. Legend gotta know what's goin' down."

Stone sucked his teeth, the weight of King Michael's words sinking in.

"Damn, Mike, that's heavy. I'll let him know Melody's... gone? And that he's got a kid he ain't even know 'bout? This gon' flip his whole world, upside down." Stone's voice dropped lower, his anger simmering just below the surface.

"I know, but it is what it is. Legend's a solider. He can handle it." Mike reasoned.

"Handling it is one thing. Him being good with the circumstances is another. You said, 'Jamaican Jay, did this right? I knew that dude was grimey, but this? Nah, they done did too much. I'll call Legend over and speak to him privately about this. We're all out here at the Thanksgiving event the girls set up, but I'll break it down to him as soon as we get off the phone. But you know this gon' turn into somethin' bigger, right? Legend ain't gon' take this layin' down, not with a son involved." Stone paused, gripping his phone tighter. "Yo, I'll handle it, but this finna get messy, Mike. Real fuckin messy."

A RATCHET CITY GOON'S THANKSGIVING CELEBRATION

The end for now...

NOTE TO READER

Dear Reader,

Thank you so much for reading my book! I sincerely hope it provided you with a memorable experience.

As a new author in the fiction genre, I rely on feedback from readers like you to grow and improve. If you enjoyed the novel, would you consider leaving a review? It can be as short or as detailed as you like. You can post it where you purchased the book or on any other review platforms you use.

Your support means the world to me and helps other readers discover my work. Thank you again for your time and your thoughts!

I love to hear any feedback about my book and enjoy interacting with my readers, so please feel free to email me at rjackson318@allureproductionsllc.com

authorrenessadjackson@gmail.com

If you would like to sign up for early notification of new releases, sign up here.

Thanks again!

Renessa D Jackson

WHAT'S NEXT ON YOUR READING LIST?

If you would like to read an unedited copy of the first chapter of the Chaos Wolf Series and the Savage Billionaire Series coming in 2025. Here is Chapter One of Chaos Wolf Ascending and A Savage Billionaire and His Ebony Queen.

Chaos Wolf Ascending
PROLOGUE Maverick Hollensworth

I paced back and forth in agitation in the center of the amphitheater surrounded by the gods who ruined my life. It was a giant monstrosity built like a Roman Colosseum with an open-air, oval shaped building with rows and rows of seats around a central area for outdoor gladiator games that seems to have been built exclusively to torture me. These bastards faked my death and broke the mating bond I had with my mate, all to bring me here to train to be able to train my daughter for some prophesized war to come in the future. They claim my sacrifice is supposed to save the world. In my opinion, fuck the world. I would have rather been there to see my daughter be born and been there to help my mate raise my son and my daughter to adulthood.

I can only imagine the hell my mate went through after losing me, then to have to go through a pregnancy alone, then birth. It's enough to drive an average person insane, and Gaia is an Alpha Wolf Guardian. The loss of a mate should have killed her, but the only exception is a pregnancy. Making her instinct to protect our pup override the need to join her mate in death. Just the thought of the pain she has been forced to endure because of my absence haunts me at night. That is on the rear occasion when I can actually sleep.

Apollo stood at the apex of the Colosseum with all the other Gods of Prophecy and War spread out around him. They all were looking at me as though I was causing them undo distress, but I don't give a fuck at this point. I have been trapped in this alternate reality for far too long. They all turned my life upside down, took my mate and children away from me and forced me into this Spartan training from the dark ages designed to shatter a person's soul in order to protect the world from the holy war they all keep harping about. It's been years since I've seen my mate and I'm passed fed the fuck up with this bullshit. Whatever else I need to learn I'll have to wing it because I'm though being their puppet.

"Apollo, why don't you let him go home now? There is nothing else we can teach him that he doesn't already know. He can best Mars, Tyr, Nyx, and Ares using both hand-to-hand combat and his various abilities. Let the man go be with his family." Morrigan spoke into the charged atmosphere.

She is the Goddess of battle and war, known as the Sovereignty Guardian Deity, who incites warriors to do battle and win gloriously even in death. Her bright orange-reddish hair sparkles in the sunlight making her pale freckled elfish face look otherworldly. Standing next to her you can feel the raw power vibrate off of her in waves. She was one of the few Gods that was against them handling things this way. Her, Phoebe, Tiresias, Brigit, Carmenta, Asclepius, and Thoth all thought I should have been allowed to stay with my mate and be trained in secret. They were all overruled by the majority, and that's why I'm here.

"Yes, Apollo. It's time. He has been here for 22 years and his daughter is an adult now. If he doesn't start teaching her how to control her abilities soon, this will all be a wasted effort. She has to learn how to control the power of Chaos are that power will consume and destroy her." Phoebe added.

Phoebe is the lunar goddess of the moon and her name means pure, bright, and prophet. Her grandchildren Apollo (Sun), and Artemis/Diana (Moon/Wolf Goddess), inherited their powers and names from her. She controls the Oracle at Delphi. She like Morrigan is a very beautiful goddess with diminutive features.

"Wait!" I shouted, "what do you mean it will consume and destroy her? None of you have ever said anything about her power being dangerous to her. You all said it was a divine power only gifted to the worthy and the

A RATCHET CITY GOON'S THANKSGIVING CELEBRATION

blessed. Nothing about her being destroyed by that power speaks of a blessing," I snapped. "Explain." I roared getting all of their attention.

Brigit approached me wearing a sympathetic expression. "Calm down, Maverick. The Power Of Chaos can kill a God and destroy the world. Of course, it's a dangerous power. That's the reason we brought you here to learn how to control it. She has the power to save and/or destroy the world. Nothing about any of this is simple, and as you know, some of us would have handled you learning how to control it differently. That's all water under the bridge now. You need to focus on what happens next," she added softly.

"Well, let's get moving. I'm way pass ready to go." I grunted, ready to get the hell away from them all, and to see my mate and children.

"That's the problem. We can't come to an agreement on what would be the best way for you to reappear, that would be believable." Carmenta explained.

She is the Goddess of childbirth and prophecy. She is the protector of mothers and their children. She is the reason for midwives and she invented the alphabet to teach reading. She was also vehemently against me being separated from my mate and children. Since the first day I arrived she has been arguing about my return up till this day.

I frowned in confusion and shook my head, "what do you mean?" I asked.

"Do we return you as Maverick Hollensworth and fake a long term stay in a hospital in a coma, or do we give you a whole new identity so you can start fresh?" Thoth asked.

Thoth is the ancient Egyptian God of the Moon, judgment, wisdom, knowledge, science, art, magic, hieroglyphs, and writing. He is often shown in art as the man standing next to Sun God Ra with the head of a baboon or ibis. Just like in the depictions of him. He has hawk like features and a predatory presence.

"I would prefer to return as myself to be with my mate and children. Whatever we have to do to make that happen, let's do it," I sighed in frustration. "Have you all forgotten I need to train my daughter? Will she trust me if I appear out the blue to train her as someone else? Forget that. I want to be with my family. I'll go back as myself. Stick me in a hospital. How did y'all explain my death anyway?" I asked.

They all exchanged guilty looks. No one would look me in the eye. I got a sick feeling in the pit of my stomach. "What the fuck did y'all do?" I yelled.

They all looked over at me as my powers burst out of me slamming into them like a tidal wave. These Gods must have forgotten that they just spent 22 years training me to kill them, and I will, or die trying if they hurt my mate and children.

Ares, Artemis, Mars, Kratos, Indra, Odin, Nyx, Tyr, and Morrigan surrounded me. I was past rational thought at this point. They have been playing games with my family's lives for years. This shit ends today.

"Maverick please calm down and listen. It's bad, but none of what happened to your wife is our fault. Let us explain." Morrigan pleaded.

I instantly calmed down. Morrigan was one of the Goddesses I trusted the most. She helped me cope with the absence of my family by giving me a small glimpse of them from time to time. It was the only thing that's got me through this torture.

I took long deep breaths fighting to get my powers back under control. It took a great amount of effort since 75% of our gifts potential output can be significantly amplified by our emotions, and these fools showed me how combining them can change and elevate them exponentially. It took me over 5 minutes to reign in the destructive power rolling out of me. Once done, I sat on the ground breathing heavily.

"Explain." I demanded.

Morrigan sat down beside me with sadness in her vibrant green eyes. She reached over and placed a reassuring hand on my arm. "It's complicated, but I will explain what we know. After you disappeared and your mate bond was severed. Your mate was forced to breed with the other three Alphas in America to strengthen the bloodlines."

"What?" I looked at her in disbelief. They all gave me sympathetic glances with varying degrees of guilt. No one but Morrigan had the guts to look me in the eye.

"Yes. After you disappeared and the mate bond was severed. The American Wolf Council got together and forced Gaia to breed with the other American Alphas. They were hoping she would have a second chance mate with one of the other alphas. She has four daughters but is still unmated. Your mate has powers no other wolf has ever possessed and they all covet that power. She is the most powerful wolf on planet Earth, second only to your daughter. The best thing is no one knows about any of your daughter's gifts. She has been hiding them

A RATCHET CITY GOON'S THANKSGIVING CELEBRATION

all except for her elemental powers that she got from both you and your mate." Tiresias explained. I looked over at him, not believing they kept all of this from me.

He is the blind prophet that transformed into a woman for years, known for his clairvoyance. He has the power to see the future.

"How could you all have kept this from me? My mate has suffered through some humiliating and horribly painful events over the past 22 years, and none of you saw fit to tell me about any of it until now," I roared. "Y'all can't be fuckin serious."

Apollo looked me in the eyes for the first time since all of this began. "Would you have been able to concentrate and learn all that you needed to learn knowing all of this was going on with your mate? No. You would have been distracted and you would have made us send you back without getting the knowledge you need to train your daughter. We did what was necessary to save this world." Apollo spewed.

"That wasn't your fucking choice to make, it was mine. My mate, my daughter, my son, our lives. You were wrong, and you know it," I spat. My power slipped from my control and Apollo flew across the ground and slammed into the far wall. His body made an indentation so deep five rows of seats were pushed back and destroyed.

Apollo pulled himself together blood coming from his eyes, nose, mouth, and ears. He walked back up to me slow and steady. You couldn't tell he'd just been magically bitch slapped.

"You done?" He asked.

I nodded, all the steam I had built up due to my anger evaporated. I just wanted to get home to my family. Everything else was irrelevant. I'm going home.

"I'm sorry these things happened. We all are, but we did what was required to save this world." He sighed and shook his head. "Let's get you home."

A Savage Billionaire and His Ebony Queen
CHAPTER ONE

Desiree stood in front of the floor length mirror situated in the corner of her room wondering where and when everything went wrong in her life. She was preparing for her 20th birthday party that was in fact nothing but a charade. Her parents were, in fact, trying to sell her off to the highest bidder, and it made her literally sick to her stomach. Just the thought that she meant nothing to them, but a high priced chess piece positioned on a board to provide them with the highest possible monetary and political gain was daunting.

They went all out planning the event to celebrate the occasion. No expense was spared and nothing but the best would be on display. Including her. What hurts the most is that the lavish event had nothing at all to do with her birthday. It was all about the so-called surprise engagement being staged. She was told to act excited when Rayvon Shaughnessy, the youngest son of State Representative Rashard Shaughnessy and Louisiana Circuit Court Judge Glenda Fisher-Shaughnessy proposed. This was a calculated move on her parents' part to link our family with the Shaughnessy family's wealth and prestige.

Our mother was known for selling her daughters to wealthy families to gain influence. It all started with the marriage of my sister Cassandra Strickland-Charles to her now husband Steven Charles 12 years ago. Steven is the heir to the prestigious Charles Investment Banking Firm. They are 3rd in line on the 10 most wealthy families in Louisiana list. Next is the marriage of our sister Rachel Strickland to Carl Grant when she was 22 years old, then William Maple at age 24, and Jack Kemp at age 28. Each of them cheated and the marriage ended in divorce.

Our sister Bridget Strickland-Miller married Chase Miller who is the heir to the Miller Textiles' Manufacturing Plant. They are the 6th richest family in Louisiana. Stephanie Strickland-Hampton, my fourth oldest sister, is married to Dewayne Hampton who is the heir to Hampton Pharmaceuticals. They are the 9th richest family in Louisiana and the deadliest. They are known to have connections to organized crime. Betty Strickland-Brooks, my fifth oldest sister is married to Jonathan Brooks airline pilot, and heir to Brooks Air-Charter Planes, and the 5th wealthiest family in Louisiana. Last is Jackie Strickland-Mims, who is married to Frank Mims Attorney, and heir to Mims and Sons Law Firm. They are the 4th wealthiest family in Louisiana and based in Baton Rouge, Louisiana.

Even with all that, I just thought things would be different for me because my parents have never once asked me to date or even entertain a man on their behalf before. So, you can imagine my surprise when my mother told me I was getting engaged to Rayvon Shaughnessy 3 days ago.

Flashback 3 days prior:

I was sitting in my parents' den with my sisters discussing our sister Rachel's latest divorce and vacation to Paris. We all felt sorry for her because all of her husbands were dogs. Each of the arranged marriages that mother set her up with has ended in divorce due to her husband's cheating. Rachel has always been a rebel and would fight mom and dad to the end, but she always did whatever they asked despite her initial protest.

"I can't believe that nigga brought a woman into their home and slept with her in Rachel's bed. That was bold as hell," Stephanie snapped. "What kind of shit is that?"

"I agree. It's the lack of respect involved in that act that I can't understand. If he wanted out of the marriage, all he had to do was ask. Rachel didn't want his lame ass in the first place. So, she would have given him a divorce with no problems." Cassandra chimed in.

"It's ridiculous. She deserved so much more than that. Especially after all she did to help him build up his practice," Bridget added.

"Y'all all seem to forget that Rachel's problem is that she is an overachiever like the rest of us. She helped to elevate each of her husband's businesses and/or statuses and then they all shitted on her because she outshined them in every way. Them nigga's egos couldn't take it. None of them nigga's deserved to be with our sister in the first place," Betty fussed. "With their jealous asses."

"That's so true," Jackie spoke up. "What's really sad is, if not for mom and dad Rachel would have married Giles straight out of college. She has been in love with that man since they first met back in high school. The only reason they are not together now is because mom and dad didn't approve of him back then. Now he's the top cardiologist in the country, and the highest paid one."

Desiree just listened to her sisters and nodded in agreement. We all knew that Rachel has been in love with Giles since forever, but she never went against our parents in matters like this. None of my sisters ever have. To be honest, I don't even think that Rachel divorced any of her husband's for cheating. It's the fact that they did it publicly that was the issue. Rachel told us that she has never been with any of her husband's sexually. So, they could fuck whoever they wanted to. They just had to keep the shit behind closed doors where it wouldn't embarrass her. Couldn't none of them stupid niggas even do that. Now that she's finally free from this last marriage. She went to get her man. I am the only one she told because she knew that I would keep her secret until after her divorce was final. She said she's done catering to mom and dad and their bullshit. It's time for her to live her own life for herself. That is if Giles is willing to forgive and forget. I believe he will because he loves Rachel just as much as she loves him.

I looked up to see mom walk in dressed to kill in a black and white Versace pants suit, black Givenchy heels, and her neck, wrist, and ears drenched in diamonds. Mom never did anything halfway. She always made sure she was the center of attention no matter what the occasion. Then with her killer body with dangerous curves to match her beautiful face she was every man's wet dream. At 52 years old mom was bad in every way and all seven of us inherited her beauty, brains, and business sense. Too bad she's a money and power-hungry monster that doesn't care who or what she has to sacrifice to get what she wants.

She stopped in front of me and paused for dramatic effect. Getting the attention of everyone at once.

"Now that I have your attention. I have an important announcement to make." She told us, grinning wide.

"What's going on Mom?" Cassy asked.

"As you all know. We will be celebrating Desiree's 20th birthday this Saturday at the Convention Center downtown," she cheesed. "Invite Only."

"Yeah. We know." Jackie chirped.

Mom gave her a glare and continued. "Well, what you don't know, is and I'm trying to tell you if you shut up. Is that it will also be Desiree's engagement announcement to Rayvon Shaughnessy." She smirked.

"What!" I shouted.

"Don't you dare take that tone with me young lady." Her mother snapped.

"I'm not trying to yell at you Mom, but I already told both you and dad that I can't stand that man. He makes my skin crawl with the way he undresses me with his eyes. That shit is creepy as hell." I screamed.

"Well, you can get over it. Your dad and I have worked hard to find you the perfect husband. He's rich, successful, and good looking. What more could you ask for?" She complained like my feelings didn't matter.

A RATCHET CITY GOON'S THANKSGIVING CELEBRATION

"I could want love, respect, companionship. I want to be with a man who sees me as more than a pretty face, and bad body. There is so much more to me than just my looks. That man is only interested in what's on the surface." I vented. Vexed at my parents lack of understanding in this situation. They act like I am purchasing a pair of shoes and not a life partner.

"Watch your tone, Desiree. I told your father that he spoiled you too much. Now you think you can do as you please, but you are dead wrong. We have already arranged this engagement and you will be there wearing a smile and looking happy when you accept his ring." She snapped and glared as she walked off.

My sisters all ran over and hugged me tight. I don't know how I was going to get out of this situation, but I refuse to marry a man I can't stand for my parent's benefit. Parents be damned.

The next day, as I sat in my room looking at the dress I was supposed to be wearing to the party. My mind drifted off to Carte. I met him when I first started high school my freshman year. I was only 14 years old at the time and he was everything I imagined my ideal man to be with his handsome muscular body. His good looks were not the only thing that made him so attractive. He was confident, dependable, supportive, hardworking, kind, committed, trustworthy, and most of all he got me on a level no one has ever before. He listened to my every word and made time to see me when I knew his time was limited. He worked every day after school and on the weekends so we were only able to spend a short amount of time together. Between him working and me hiding our relationship from my family, our time was confined to our lunch breaks at school and stolen moments on the weekend. Those brief periods of time we were together meant everything to me because I got to know exactly what it felt like to be loved and cherished by a man.

Since I was only 14 and Carte was 17 years old. There was a limit to what we could do as a couple, and due to that. I got to know him in a completely platonic way. I would watch him at practice for the basketball and football teams, and he would watch me at track practice. He would help me with my homework, so I was able to find out that he is incredibly smart. I even met and got to know his Aunt Connie who is his closest relative and most important person. Even now, she and I talk at least once or twice a week.

Carte has been gone for over 6 years without a word to me, and I still regret what happened when he came to see me after his graduation from high school. He stopped by our house, knocked on the door and asked to speak with me. I had no idea he'd been by until my mom came into my room and questioned me about what I was doing with that thug. I honestly didn't know what she was talking about because she didn't mention Carte's name and the person she described sounded nothing like him. That coupled with the fact that Carte had no idea where I lived made me believe it couldn't possibly have been him. Little did I know a week later I found out from the maid he'd been by when she showed me a picture of him that she'd discreetly taken with her phone. She told me how mom tried to embarrass him by telling him he wasn't good enough for me. I was so hurt because when I later saw him before he left and tried to apologize on my mother's behalf. He thought it was out of pity and not the genuine affection I have for him. I love that man and he is the only man I plan to be with.

Now I just have to find a way to get out of this stupid ass engagement. I will be going to the party and putting up with all the bells and whistles to keep up appearances, but I'm not marrying anyone other than Carte Blanche-Powell.

Coming out of her daydream. Desiree did a last minute check on her make-up and hair that was styled to perfection for this occasion by the top MUA and hairstylist in the city. Mom even went so far as to pick out my outfit. I can't complain since she chose a Vera Wang strapless black mini dress made of lace silk with black pearls throughout. It gave new meaning to the classic little black dress. She paired the dress with red bottom peep toe Christian Louboutin heels and the matching clutch tote. I kept the jewelry to a minimum with string chandelier diamond earrings with the matching necklace and bracelet. No rings. The total look came together well. Now I just have to keep the touching to a minimum.

DESIREE LET OUT A LONG breath and went to meet her parents in the foyer under the double staircase. Her mother scrutinized her appearance from head to toe. Her father tried to make small talk to relieve some of the tension in the air, but she had nothing to say to either of them. The drive to the

A RATCHET CITY GOON'S THANKSGIVING CELEBRATION

convention center was strained, with the atmosphere in the limo oozing with toxicity and Desiree couldn't wait to get the hell away from both of them. After the 30 minute drive, the limo pulled up to the curb and the driver got out and opened the door for us to get. Desiree was the first one out of the door walking quickly down the red carpet. She didn't pause for photos with the photographers lined up outside to take pictures. She could feel her mother's dark glare on her back as she made her way to her sisters and their husbands standing off to the side of the entranceway. They were all wide eyed, not believing she left their parents and walked off not bothering to pose for a single picture, but they hadn't seen anything yet. Desiree refused to cooperate with this shit show. No one was selling her. She was not for sale.

As soon as she made it within touching distance Cassy grabbed her arm and pulled her to the side. "What are you doing Desiree?" She hissed. "Mom and dad are going to be pissed. I can see it in her eyes. She's mad as hell."

"She'll get over it, because I don't give a fuck. I'm not their property to sell off to the highest bidder. Fuck them!" She exclaimed.

Briddy pulled me away from Cassy. "Calm down Desiree. I know you're upset, but this is not the time nor place for this. Let's just get through the party and we can discuss your options later."

"Yeah, Desiree. We all know you are upset, but let's not make things worse by acting out. Let's get through tonight first. We can deal with the fallout later," Betty added and the rest of them nodded in agreement.

Desiree gave them all a stiff nod, took a deep breath, and put on a fake smile. They all watched and waited for their parents to take pictures for all the reporters and answered a few questions. When their parents walked up Desiree didn't miss the menacing glare her mother threw her way. She rolled her eyes at her mom, eliciting yet another stony look, but Desiree wasn't fazed. She couldn't believe her mother had the nerve to be upset after the shit she set in motion.

Her father walked over and patted her hand. "You okay baby girl?" He asked.

Desiree looked into his eyes wondering if he was really okay with her mother trying to marry her off to that pervert. She couldn't tell if he was concerned about her wellbeing or his public image. She just nodded her head and headed through the double doors following the rest of the family.

The hall was well decorated and all of the who's who were present tonight. The Mayors of Shreveport and of Bossier, Governor, State Representatives Shaughnessy and Caldwell, Senators Givens and Delaney, District Attorney Lorian, Judges Parks, Franklin and McMillen, lawyers, doctors, and other elite businessmen all came out with their families to help Desiree celebrate her birthday. Everyone was here to rub elbows and be seen with the top 15% of the elite class. There were tastefully designed banners with Happy Birthday Desiree hung in different sections of the banquet hall. It all looked nice, but Desiree took no pleasure in the event, knowing she was not the real reason for the celebration. It all left a bad taste in her mouth.

Mom and Dad switched to business mode and went off to mingle. Desiree hung out with her sisters and their husbands. Most of whom were conversing with their families and other business colleagues. That lasted until her feet started hurting in her heels and Jackie caught her limping and suggested they all take a break in the rest area on the second floor of the Convention Center containing the lounge sofas and chairs. We were all looking forward to getting off our feet in these heels, when we approached the cracked lounge door and heard a familiar voice coming from inside.

"That's my spot, right there daddy. Give it to me harder. Harder!" We all heard and exchanged a shocked glance, grinning.

"Keep your voice down. I'm not trying to get caught up in here with you." Desiree heard Rayvon Shaughnessy say as she and her sisters burst through the lounge door.

Rayvon had a half-naked woman bent over the back of the sofa sectional with the bottom half of her dress pulled up to her waist and the top half pushed down to her waist. Leaving both the top and bottom halves of her body completely exposed. From the angle from the door, we could all see Rayvon's condom covered dick gyrating in and out of her in rapid succession. He looked up and saw us standing there and didn't even break his stride to acknowledge our presence. If anything, it seemed like it made his dick get harder so he started to fuck her with complete abandonment.

Desiree shook her head at his audacity. "I wouldn't marry your sick ass if you were the last nigga on earth, and my life depended on it. I'd die first."

A RATCHET CITY GOON'S THANKSGIVING CELEBRATION

He had the nerve to bite down on his tongue and lick his lips, while giving Desiree a long lingering appraisal from head to toe. The shit was turning him on. Lust bloomed in his eyes and they slid to slits.

"Let's get out of here Desiree. Once we tell mom and dad about this, I'm sure they will call this bullshit marriage off." Cassy told me as we all headed back out the door.

"I wouldn't count on it. You will be mine Desiree. One way or another. You can bet on that." Rayvon chuckled, and fuck ole girl even harder before shouting, "close the door."

We all rushed back down the stairs and told dad what happened. He rushed up the stairs with mom following close behind him. Shortly afterwards State Representative Shaughnessy and his wife rushed up the stairs. My sisters and I made our way around the hall speaking to people we knew, trying to salvage what we could of the remainder of my birthday celebration. While greeting the guest, I saw Casey, Krystal, and Samantha grinning while watching the stairs. I made my way over to greet them and let them know we were going to head out. Before I even got the chance to speak, Casey said some shit that rubbed me the wrong way.

"Desiree, I noticed your parents and the Shaughnessy's haven't come back downstairs yet. Is there something going on?" She asked in a voice dripping with sarcasm.

"Why I don't know Casey. Maybe you can tell me what you think is going on, since you tend to think you know everything anyway." Desiree used reverse sarcasm.

"Don't be like that Desiree. We all saw you and your sisters rushing downstairs to talk to your parents. Then they rushed upstairs followed by the Shaughnessy's. Something important must have happened, and we're all a little curious." Casey clarified.

"Casey, you do know that curiosity killed the cat. Right? Are you trying to die?" Desiree asked, looking directly into her eyes.

"Desiree let's go. I don't know why you're even still entertaining this hoe. You know she's green with envy where you are concerned. She can't stand that you're better than she is at everything. You need to cut her jealous ass off. For good." Jackie groused.

"Jealous! What do I have to be jealous of? Desiree is no better than me, and what's up with the name calling? That's uncalled for." Casey snapped.

"Careful with that tone, chilly. You know you want to be Desiree so bad you can't stand it. Everything she gets, you just have to have one or something similar to it. Every nigga that's ever liked Desiree you have tried to get. Even with y'all fake ass friends you have to be the center of attention. The only thing that ruins that for you is that you can't compete with my sister and you always end up with cake on your face." Betty taunted.

Desiree shook her head, not in the mood to go back and forth with Casey today. "I'll talk to y'all later. We're leaving, but you all can stay and enjoy yourselves. The party's not nearly over yet. So, eat, drink, and enjoy," Desiree told them and followed her sisters out with their husbands.

"I can't stand them bitches. They all think they are more than everyone else because they were married into the wealthiest and most influential families." Casey vented once Desiree and her sisters were out of earshot.

"You know the shit you just said would have had more of an impact if you would have said it to their faces instead of behind their backs?" Krystal asked.

"Are you trying to be funny?" Casey hissed.

"No. I'm trying to be real. I ain't none of Samantha kissing your ass. My family is good and I don't need your crumbs. You talk a lot of shit when Desiree ain't around but be on mute when you are in her face. That shit is foul, and I ain't finna bite my tongue to cater to you." Krystal shot back.

"Y'all need to stop. But Casey Krystal is right. You already know how Desiree's sisters are about her, and you still are saying stuff to make them go off. You need to stop doing that shit. We are all friends so the backbiting needs to stop." Samantha added.

Casey didn't say anything more, just watching Desiree and her sisters as they made their way out of the Convention Center. "I still wonder what's going on." She thought.

STAY CONNECTED

@
Join My Email List

Stay up to date with everything happening in Renessa D. Jackson's world-including new releases, upcoming releases, sales, updates, giveaways, events, and more.

Newsletter Link

authorrenessadjackson@gmail.com

CONNECT ON SOCIAL

X
https://x.com/Allure_Pro_LLC?t=BmAST0NE7pOAgwoMk_v6KA&s=09

Snapchat
https://www.snapchat.com/add/allure_prollc?share_id=XZnXibghlIk&locale=en-US

Instagram
https://www.instagram.com/allure_productions_llc/

TikTok
https://www.tiktok.com/@allure_productions_llc?lang=en

YouTube
https://www.youtube.com/@AllureProductionsPresentsRenes

Website
https://allureproductionsllc.com/

Renessa D. Jackson Ratchet City Readers Facebook Group
https://www.facebook.com/groups/2070696710014497

ABOUT THE AUTHOR

Renessa D. Jackson, a native of Shreveport, LA, was born under the vibrant sign of Aries in April. Her temperament personifies the bright optimism and meticulous organization that her zodiac sign suggests. Her journey through life's challenges has molded her into a determined and confident leader, traits that shine through in every aspect of her personal and professional endeavors.

Renessa's love affair with reading began in her twenties, sparked by the captivating worlds of Manga and Manhwa. This initial spark soon grew into a blazing passion that includes fanfiction, romance, and urban fiction. Today, she finds joy in exploring a wide array of genres, immersing herself in the diverse and rich narratives that books provide.

Her deep appreciation for literature seamlessly translates into her own writing. As an author, Renessa is excited to welcome readers into the vivid and dynamic stories that have been brewing in her imagination. "Luvin a Young Ratchet City Boss," her debut novel, marks the beginning of the Ratchet City Boss series, promising many more enthralling tales to come.

Contributing to her bustling life, Renessa is surrounded by a loving family, including her six children, grandchildren and host of extended family members and friends.

Renessa continues to call Shreveport Louisiana home, where she is a cherished and active member of the literary community. She treasures the connections she makes with fellow authors and readers who share her passion for storytelling.

ABOUT THE PUBLISHER

Allure Productions LLC is a dynamic publishing company dedicated to bringing powerful, authentic stories to life. Specializing in urban fiction and diverse narratives, we're passionate about amplifying unique voices and delivering captivating tales that resonate with readers. From raw street fiction to heartwarming romances, Allure Productions strives to publish stories that inspire, entertain, and connect with audiences on a personal level. With a commitment to quality and creativity, we're building a platform where compelling stories find their way into the hands of book lovers everywhere.

ACKNOWLEDGEMENT

I would like to extend my heartfelt thanks to Carla Hill and my Ratchet City Readers and everyone else who took the time to read my book and provide honest feedback and constructive tips for improvement.

Special thanks to Jonessa Johnson for enduring my wild mood swings and the numerous changes to the cover.

I am immensely grateful to Dr. Dee Davis for assisting with all the technical details that I worried about completing on time.

Shut out to Jaylen Davis for helping me with advertising on the different social media platforms. He is a lifesaver because I am lost in the social media world.

I would like to give a very special thanks to Byron Allen, the owner of the Fresh2Def87 Barber & Beauty Shop on Pierre Avenue and Miliam Street over in the Lakeside Allendale Subdivision. There are many out there that know and love his skills with the clippers and his fresh style of dress.

Lastly, I would like to thank my cover model Rondicious Davis and graphic designer Jonessa Johnson for their patience with my steadfast resolve to remain genuine in my presentation.